"Bickering parents, weird sex, and ambiguous floral arrangements pave the road to enlightenment in legendary comedy writer Merrill Markoe's first novel. . . . Along the way she reminds readers that the heart is a fragile little critter. And sometimes the best we can do is make a wish and blow those candles out."
—*O magazine*

"A dark, witty story about one woman's attempt to find the right man and not kill her mother."
—*Talk*

"Witty . . . Markoe's very funny and astute about women's insecurities."
—*The Hartford Courant*

"Perfect for curling up with at the end of the day when we long for the company of good friends, but they've all gone to bed. You know, after watching the *Late Show*."
—*St. Petersburg Times*

"Laugh-out-loud debut fiction . . . classy stuff that deserves tons of flowers from dazed and satisfied readers."
—*Kirkus Reviews*

"[Markoe] brings her crisp, gratifyingly feminist sense of humor and flair for satirizing the lives of frustrated singles to an irresistible first novel."
—*Booklist*

"The perfect gift for all women who face birthdays with grim determination, pepper spray and sharp fingernail files . . . Markoe teaches the joy of laughing through pain and bubbling through toil and trouble."
—*Publishers Weekly*

It's My F---ing Birthday

It's My F---ing Birthday

A NOVEL

Merrill Markoe

VILLARD
NEW YORK

2003 Villard Books Trade Paperback Edition

Copyright © 2002 by Merrill Markoe

All rights reserved under International and Pan-American Copyright Conventions. Published in the United States by Villard Books, a division of Random House, Inc., New York, and simultaneously in Canada by Random House of Canada Limited, Toronto.

Villard Books and "V" Circled Design are registered trademarks of Random House, Inc.

This work was originally published in hardcover in 2002 by Villard Books, a division of Random House, Inc.

Library of Congress Cataloging-in-Publication Data
Markoe, Merrill.
It's my f---ing birthday: a novel
p. cm.
ISBN 0-8129-6724-0
1. Women art teachers—Fiction.   2. Parent and adult child—Fiction.
3. Dating (Social customs)—Fiction.   4. Los Angeles (Calif.)—Fiction.
5. Birthdays—Fiction.   I. Title.
PS3563.A6652 I87 2002
813'.54—dc21   2001049242

Villard Books website address: www.villard.com

Printed in the United States of America

68975

Book design by Casey Hampton

To Lewis, Bo, Tex, Winky, Corey, and Noah—
six of my favorite guys

Acknowledgments

Thanks to: Melanie Jackson and Bruce Tracy. And also to Polly Draper, Todd Hansen, Mavis Jukes Hudson, Susan Jaffee, Maudey Jaffee, Glenn Markoe, Andy Prieboy, Maria Semple, Robin Schiff, and Space Ghost.

It's My F---ing Birthday

Thirty-six

WELL, IT'S MY FUCKING BIRTHDAY AGAIN. One year ago today I remember being so sure that this was the year that everything would turn around. I could sense it. I could feel it in the air. But here I am, a full year later, just as screwed up as ever, still making the same mistakes over and over. So I am initiating a new tradition. My plan is to carefully scrutinize my past in the name of not being condemned to repeat it by writing myself an annual report on my birthday. Kind of a personal state of the union to help me chart my profits and losses or at least get a clearer picture of what I am doing right and wrong. I'm not stupid enough to think it's going to keep me from making mistakes ever again but it would be nice if at least I could start making some new ones.

Okay. So, still living alone. Still an art teacher and still not minding it too bad. Although I wouldn't have believed it possible when I turned thirty, turning thirty-six doesn't feel like that much of a nightmare. And what more could a thirty-six-year-old girl mired in the quicksand of the one-year anniversary of a painful breakup want on her birthday than a long day of sulking, followed by a chance to go out to dinner with her narcissistic mother and father? Nothing eases the pain of a searing depression like the joy of watching one's elderly parents pick petty fights in upscale restaurants.

As always, the fun started the minute we were seated at a table in a pleasant little bistro near the ocean called Kettle'O'Fish (which I ordinarily would have condemned based on the 'O' thing but it was actually pretty nice). My mother took one look at the complimentary tureen of crudités being placed before us, gave the smiling waitress a withering glance, and said, "That's a very meager amount, isn't it?" The waitress stared blankly for a few seconds, picked up the crudité arrangement, and took it back into the kitchen, where probably every member of the staff pissed or spit on it before she brought it back a carrot stick or two heavier. I, of course, sat quietly cringing like I used to do in the seventh grade, only too aware that neither of my two options provided me with any solace: to invoke the wrath of my mother by daring to criticize her or to sit in quiet humiliation, doing a little out-of-body traveling, pretending to enjoy balmy breezes in Bora Bora.

"So what if everyone in this restaurant hates my mother?" I could say to myself unconvincingly. "I'm used to that by now. A lifetime of such incidents have enabled me to produce antibodies that process the bodily fluids of restaurant employees into beneficial dietary supplements, like riboflavin or vitamin B_{12}."

I could also harbor the tiniest glimmer of hope that the jury was still out, among those who would condemn us, on my father. It was possible that maybe the waiters and waitresses might think I was his child from a previous marriage.

However, what my father lacked in active vitriol, he compensated for with sheer arrogance. His tenacious grasp of the obvious had long ago given him the impression that as the bearer of a superior intellect it was both his duty and his burden to patiently explain even the simplest processes of daily living to nearly everyone he met, not just once but every occasion that they met. Which is why my birthday lunch found him lecturing the busboy in excruciating detail on the preferred way to pour water from a pitcher.

"Listen to me carefully so I don't have to eat my damn lunch soaking wet," he began. "If you don't hold that pitcher with two hands how the hell do you expect to get any directional stability when you pour?"

If I'd *ever* used that tone of voice on any of the kids in the high school classes I've taught, I would have received enough dramatically incensed exhalations to be pushed across the room like a sailboat in a hurricane.

Next it was back to my place for the annual celebratory birthday drink, a pleasant yearly ritual that I almost ruined for them both by not knowing about the water spots on my champagne glasses. This, of course, sent my mother into a tailspin. When she finally recovered from the nightmare of being exposed to potentially life-threatening bacteria during a visit to her own daughter's house, and the rewashed glasses were polished to an almost terrifying state of cleanliness, the champagne was dispensed by my father with one of his patented two-handed pours. That's when my mother offered her annual toast.

oming year," she said, hoisting her blindingly clean
ng glass into the air, "may half of all your dreams

"Mom," I said to her, "isn't that kind of pathetic?"

"Well, it's realistic," she said, taking a sip of champagne and staring into the middle distance.

No point in ignoring harsh realities in a birthday toast, I thought to myself, realizing that she had given me something for which I should be grateful. Because if realism was her point, she *could* have said, "May half of all your dreams die a horrible death."

Then she did her part to make sure I didn't score better than 50 percent in the dream department this particular birthday by giving me yet another piece of clothing there was no chance I would ever wear in this or any other lifetime: an unstructured floor-length velveteen tunic with a gold rope belt and gold braid trim, a kind of high-fashion Greco-Roman monastic sheath.

In addition to being inappropriate, it also succeeded in making me sad that my mother was still energetically continuing her tradition of wasting time every single year searching out and buying me things that were not my taste, especially since she never failed to follow up the gift bestowal by telling me how much she paid for the garment in question, I guess to ensure that it would receive the respect to which it was planning to grow accustomed.

"This is not an inexpensive dress" is how she began this year. By the third glass of champagne she worked in the exact dollar amount, disguised as special care and cleaning instructions. "Be sure and get this dry-cleaned," she said as offhandedly as she could. "It's a two-hundred-and-sixty-dollar item."

This was my father's cue to begin his lengthy semiannual lecture on how to correctly remove wrapping paper from a gift.

"If you take the time to remove the tape slowly, the entire wrapping paper comes off in one big, untorn sheet." He demonstrated, as though performing a trick for a poorly attended after-school magic show. "Just follow your creases carefully and it folds back up nice and flat." I wore the same expression I'd been perfecting for decades, carefully constructed to convey such a visible amount of real comprehension that my father would feel no need to repeat himself. There was, of course, no chance at all that this would happen.

But the best was still ahead—the part where my mother insisted I try her gift on for them and provide a little fashion show. It has become an annual high-water mark for my feelings of self-loathing, an annual opportunity to see myself looking older, and fatter, and uglier all at once than I have at any other moment of the year. This year, when I caught a glimpse of myself in the window behind the very sofa on which my parents were sitting, I reminded myself of a bulldog who had just come home from the groomer with a bow tied around her neck. I looked like I was trying very hard to be something I was never intended to be, and failing in the most embarrassing way possible. I felt like Janet Reno in a fluffy ball gown.

Happy Birthday to me.

By now, my mother was deeply into full-out gush, showering me with the only compliments she ever offered me in fiscal '92.

"See?" she said to my father. "She never buys the feminine styles. But look how lovely she can look if she wants to." My father agreed, or pretended to agree. I could never tell if he was paying attention.

They were soul mates, my mother and father. They claimed to adore each other, as if the word "adore" meant "argue with ceaselessly." And although they criticized and demeaned each other as much as they demeaned me, they lived in a weird little universe only big enough for two that was impermeable to criticism unless they were delivering it.

During these birthday moments it seemed as if everything positive I had ever honestly perceived about myself was incorrect. All I could do was stand there running a quick scan in my brain of the easiest, most trouble-free, cost-effective methods for killing myself.

As I saw it, I could take every pill in the medicine cabinet, without even knowing what pills were in there exactly. Would a whole bottle of Sudafed bring a painless death sentence? What about twenty-five Zoloft? If they didn't kill me, might they at least provide enough relaxation to give me the courage to stumble out to the car with a hose and suck up exhaust?

Oh sure, the folks would be all upset at first. But eventually they would turn it into a long, pointless, puzzling anecdote that would give them a certain distinction among their friends as survivors of tragedy.

Tragedy carried a lot of weight as entertainment among their peers. Tragedy and pointless details, like the way Dad was able to reduce the impressive world traveling he and my mother did regularly to anecdotes of no real interest. How often had I heard him tell the tale of his trip to Turkey where his unexpected breakfast egg order at the Istanbul Hilton had shattered all expectations?

"I almost always get the poached eggs," he would explain, not as surprised as he should have been that the people he was talking to were still awake. "I like them scrambled but a lot of hotels make them too damn greasy."

"I'd been telling him for years he'd like the three-minute eggs if he'd just try them," my mother would pipe in, "but just try talking *him* into *anything*!"

"Anyway, long story short, I don't know what it was about being in Turkey. . . . But I ordered the three-minute eggs. And P.S. . . . I've been eating them ever since!"

Maybe next trip to Turkey he would really cut loose and order the Spanish omelette. Or maybe he'd be willing to tell me that story one last time while I wrapped a sock around my neck and hung myself out the window.

Even though some of this continuing pursuit of the marginal annoyed my mother, she was still able to enjoy it in her own way. They shared a real fixation on food. Sometimes when we were alone together as a family, that was the only topic of conversation she would permit. She'd want to know what I had eaten, and when. What I had at home in my cupboard. Why I always ordered the same things at restaurants. What I favored for snacks. Why I didn't cook more. What my friends ate for dinner. Why I didn't eat more halibut and less salmon. Whether or not I still disliked brussels sprouts, or sardines, or beets. Why I didn't make all the same choices she did.

So these were my parents, the people put on earth to judge me, to advise me, to correct me, to mold me in their image. And they took these tasks very, very seriously, even as I was turning thirty fucking six.

And just when I was pretty sure that a birthday celebration couldn't get any more dismal, there was a knock on the door. Standing outside was a young man holding a huge glass container of flowers: an enormous mixed spring assortment of dahlias, daisies, ranunculuses, tulips, zinnias, daffodils, and pink roses. The vase was so heavy I could hardly take it from him. My brain raced through a Rolodex of names and addresses, trying to figure out who sent them.

Nervously, I read the card. "Happy Birthday Carl," it said flatly, almost as though the flowers were for him. I felt a jolt go through me as the information registered. The blood drained from my face. I felt queasy and light-headed.

I thanked the delivery person and walked crablike across the room, carrying a vase that weighed as much as an eight-year-old child. I placed the giant cauldron of flowers on the dining-room table, then sat down and started to cry.

This was the first communication from Carl since our final "fuck-yous" a year ago. What, if anything, was sending flowers on my birthday supposed to mean? Not just flowers, mind you, but a behemoth expensive bouquet? Did it mean "I miss you" or "I still love you"? Was he trying to say "Please don't hate me forever"?

Carl was never the kind of guy who gave a gift much thought. One year he bought himself two men's tennis shirts and, when he realized it was my birthday, gave one to me as a present. He probably just yelled the flower idea out the door to his secretary. I wondered if she had picked out the type of flowers.

That he had so often forgotten my birthday when we were together made it all the more puzzling that he remembered it now.

And what exactly was I supposed to do? Call him and tell him all was forgiven? Send a thank-you note, indicating I was willing to overlook all the bad air still circulating between us?

Or did he want to hear remorse over seven years that had gone up in sulfurous smoke? One expensive bouquet of flowers and now I was supposed to think it's a brand fucking new world for us to share? He had already yanked some tears out of me without my permission and now here I was obsessing on the psychological origins of his behavior as a way to seem more detached than I really was. I was secretly terrified that the dumb girl inside me might want him back.

I think, at least I certainly hope, that not even the dumb girl *really* wanted him back. He was the asshole in this. He was the liar and the cheater. I was so lucky he didn't call me. And the dumb girl was even luckier.

I mean, even if he did call, what the fuck did he want me to say? "It's okay that you jerked me around and treated me like shit. Now that I have received this enormous bouquet of seasonal flowers, I am beginning to see you in a very different light. Suddenly the past is growing hazy. All the hateful things you did and said have grown distant and hard to recall. So if you want to come by for some coffee or a drink at your convenience, I would love to say hello and give you a *blow job!*"

I have high hopes that this will be the year the dumb girl in me finally dies. She is long overdue for a painless, or even a painful, death. I'm so sick of listening to her try to convince me of things I know don't make any sense: that the plots of romantic movies are plausible; that men who have cheated repeatedly might suddenly decide to turn over a new leaf; that guys who are assholes might turn out to be more considerate in time.

I think I have been afraid to kill her completely because I'm worried that she's the only one of us who still has a little hope. I think I've been counting on her hope and her naïveté to keep me from falling into the Hole. The Hole is what I worry about. I'm at the age where I notice that an awful lot of women fall into the Hole. All these nice, smart, fun, attractive women in their late thirties and upward—sitting in there, whining, moaning, hoping for escape. And for the most part, they aren't quite sure what happened to cause them to take the tumble. But once they have fallen in, they can't seem to find a way out again.

So they just sit in there, comparing notes on what went wrong.

"Why are you in here?"

"Well, I was married for thirteen years but ever since the divorce, I just can't seem to make anything work. Why are you in here?"

"Who me? Well, I'm not sure. I just never meet anyone appealing anymore. It's been three years since my last date. Four years since I had sex."

And there they all sit. In the Hole. Hoping someone will show up with a ladder. Watching all day long, just staring up at the edge. Discussing other ways to get out but not really thinking of any. Just sitting quietly, trying to remain calm, imagining things they might do to dress up the Hole interior. Waiting, waiting, waiting for someone to throw them a rope.

So I know I have to do what I can, not to fall into that Hole with them. I know I have to be very, very careful.

But it's equally if not more dangerous to let the dumb girl assert too much influence over my behavior. I'm sure if I let her, she would make the case that no one sends flowers for a birthday a year after a nasty breakup unless they were moved by serious feelings. And I would have to waste my time sitting her down to remind her that this is just another amazing facsimile of a sincere emotional gesture. Like the day he was supposedly so emotionally devastated by the death of his grandmother that he didn't have the energy to speak to me, let alone attend his grandmother's funeral. I was a crazy, selfish, cold bitch who didn't understand how truly devastated he was. Yet he was somehow miraculously able to pull himself together long enough to spend the day playing golf and basketball with his buddies, and then later go to a hockey game and out to a sports bar for a couple of beers.

"Not this shit again," said my dad, as he watched me grow weepy over the flowers. "I thought we were done with this crap already. It's been a year. People meet, get married, change jobs, have a kid, and file for a divorce in the course of a year. Meanwhile you just hang around mired in the same old shit." He didn't buy the equation from the women's magazines that it takes half the time the relationship lasted to fully recover.

"So you don't have anyone special you're seeing?" my mother piped in, with such exhaustion and despair that I couldn't let it pass without a comment.

"Well, no," I said, trying to create the impression that I couldn't really care less. My mother gave me a long, lingering look.

"I could say something but I'm not going to say anything. I know you will just jump down my throat," she said, looking at me and then looking away.

"Well, Mom, now that you've said *that,* you might as well say what you were not going to say," I said, irritated at myself for taking the bait.

"Oh, no," she said, "no way I'm walking into that trap. Nooo."

"Why did you bring it up *at all* if you're not going to say it?" I asked, exasperated.

"I don't think you have any interest in what I have to say," she said. "What does it matter what I say? I'm just your dumb old mother. What the hell could I possibly know?"

I sat there fuming, not really knowing what move to make next. It was a scenario similar to ones I endured with petulant students. In those instances it was always up to me to rise above the fray. In this instance it was the only option as well.

"Well, Mom, you know that's not true. Of course I care what you have to say," I said, never wanting to hear anything she had to say ever again.

"No, you don't," she said, staring off wistfully.

"Yes I do. I do too," I said, hating myself for being in this conversation in the first place, but not knowing how to get out of it. Wishing I could be teleported back in time to that precious moment before I stepped in my mother's emotional gum wad.

"Well," she said, taking a long pause, "there are certain things a woman can do to make herself more appealing. . . ."

"And what would those be, Mom?" I asked, feeling a rage building inside me. "Teach me how to get stuck in a lifelong rut with someone who will argue with every single thing I say like you do with Dad" is what I really wanted to say. Although I had already learned that lesson. That was the relationship I'd had with Carl.

"Obviously you don't want to hear what I have to say," she replied.

"Yes, I do," I said to her. "The only thing I don't want is a scalding critique of how awful you think I look."

"Fine," she said, staring off into the middle distance, appearing lost in a nonspecific but very painful memory. "I can't talk to you about anything anymore. Everything I say is wrong."

And with that she got up and went into the adjoining room, to stare up at the ceiling.

"I don't know why you have to do this to your mother every time we get together," said my father, rising to go comfort her. "What is it with you anyway?"

A short while later the happy couple left.

I went into the dining room, sat down in the seat my mother had vacated, and stared at the flowers myself. They really, really made me sad. I guess I wouldn't have had such a dramatic reaction if I had some other love life to distract me. But in fiscal '92, the only other romantically linked experience I had was that weird guy from the acting class: the one whose name I keep blanking out on purpose. I don't even know if you can file that episode into the romance category.

I only signed up for that class as a way to get out of the house. "You have to get *out* there," people kept saying to me. "Out *where?*" I would answer them back. "*Where* am I supposed to go?" And then for lack of a specific location, I decided to try and take some classes.

I met Keith almost the minute I walked into the little theater where the class met. He was cute in an eight-by-ten glossy kind of a way. He struck me as an underachiever from another part of the country who felt his looks entitled him to a part on *Beverly Hills 90210*. All he had to do was learn a little bit about acting in order to be eligible for his profile in *People* magazine.

That first class he took off his shirt every chance he got. We had to do an improvisation where everyone had to play an animal. He played a shirtless Doberman pinscher, followed by a shirtless raccoon.

He showed up at the second class armed with a scene he wanted us to perform together. I don't know why he picked me. I didn't think my llama had gone over particularly well.

The scene he brought was a couple in bed, arguing after making love. It had everything: sex, anger, a very long pretentious speech for him, many reasons for shirtlessness.

I shrugged and said, "Sure." Because I was flattered he asked. He winked and said he would call to arrange a rehearsal.

The very next day the L.A. Riots started. Los Angeles was on fire. Whole streets were cordoned off. Rioters were looting and fighting and being videotaped doing both. The television news was showing live coverage of otherwise ordinary-looking citizens breaking the plate-glass windows in the front of stores, then struggling to carry a heavy dishwasher or a cumbersome dinette set down the street. They looked busy but chillingly nonchalant, as though they had bagged an elk during hunting season and now had the inconvenient task of trying to get the carcass home. As though stealing a heavy appliance out of a store was a burdensome but necessary chore that they had no choice but to try and manage with a certain amount of good nature.

It was a frightening glimpse into the dark, jagged hole that was in the center of the make-believe culture that apparently wasn't really holding the city of Los Angeles together after all. I sat petrified, wondering if I was in danger. Wondering what might happen next.

And of course what happened next was that the phone rang. It was Keith, wanting to rehearse. "What are you doing right now?" he asked me.

"Watching the last moments of civilization crumble on my TV," I said, immediately realizing he might think I meant I was watching Sally Jesse Raphaël, so I clarified.

"Have you seen the riot coverage at all?" I asked him. I couldn't take my eyes off the set. I was watching breathlessly, terrified.

"No," he said, "I don't watch TV."

"You might want to turn it on," I said. "The city is coming apart live on camera before our very eyes. Everything everywhere seems to be on fire."

"I was wondering if now would be an okay time for me to come over and run lines?" he asked, as if the earlier portion of our conversation had never taken place.

At first I was stunned by his disinterest in the destruction of our mutual hometown, by his unique ability to maintain total self-absorption in the face of disaster. But the riot had succeeded in making me such a paranoid mess, I decided that as long as he was willing to drive to my house, I would rather not be alone.

He had his shirt off almost before he came in the door. He actually suggested that we both needed to take off all our clothes and get into bed to get our motivation right. I said no. So then he wanted to tie me to a chair and try the scene bondage-style. When I declined again, he wanted to lie on top of me or have me sit on his lap or he would sit on top of me.

The possibilities were endless, as long as they involved full-body physical contact and partial nudity. I said no a dozen times at least.

Finally all the manic sexual energy he was sending my way started to get to me. His eyes looked like a comic-book drawing of someone with X-ray vision.

I didn't plan on having sex with him. But of course soon I found myself thinking, *Why not have sex? What else do I have to do anyway? His acting sucks. This scene is doomed no matter how good I am. And this has got to be a better approach to living than sitting around moping about Carl. This will at least put some distance in between me and the breakup and my feelings and my sadness.* Because of the riots, everything had a kind of a *Diary of Anne Frank* tone that made it all a little more compelling.

And so it came to pass that he and I had sex while the city of Los Angeles was burning. Or should I say, I had his version of sex with him.

Afterward all I could think of was that at last he had provided me with a clear definition of what I meant by really, really, *really* bad sex. Not only was I not turned on, but he had no idea whatsoever where the parts he needed to make contact with were located on me. Instead, his technique seemed to be: pick a random location and begin rubbing it in the hope that a clitoris would eventually grow out of all the unnecessary friction.

Here was a guy who claimed to earn his living as a handyman. He could take an engine apart. He could rewire a dishwasher. He could reroof a house. But he had no idea at all where anything was on a woman. If he wired a car the same way he made love, the windows would open and close when he put his foot on the accelerator. And where oral sex was con-

19

cerned, it was kind of like he got on the 101 meaning to exit at Lankershim and instead got off at Laurel Canyon. So near and yet so far away. I'm being kind: He wasn't really even as close as a missed freeway exit.

But it was not until the second time that he rammed my head into the wall behind my bed that I decided to call a halt to the proceedings. He was bouncing and jiggling me as though I was a pair of ill-fitting pants that he was trying to force up over his hips. He was grunting and sweating and making faces that reminded me of the primitive man exhibit at the Museum of Natural History. Although I must say, he deserved some kind of special honors for his unique hyenalike noises. I'd never heard anything remotely like them before.

As I watched him, I tried to memorize every single detail with as much clinical detachment as I could so I would never ever make this same mistake again.

By then I realized that since there was going to be no way to stop him I might as well cooperate by doing a little orgasm faking in the hopes that maybe this would make things end more quickly. That, of course, was a mistake since reinforcement of any kind was a very bad idea. Once we hit the point where brevity was out of the question, my irritation with him became so extreme that the only thing I could think of was to tell him I thought I was going to vomit. That got his attention. He dismounted politely, allowing me to run into the bathroom and shut the door. As I sat alone on the toilet, with the water running to give the impression of important activity, I had never been so grateful to be alone in my entire life.

When I finally reemerged I was more than delighted to note he had already put on his pants. Words cannot adequately describe how truly happy his repantsing made me.

"Are you feeling better now?" he asked, as though he was considering resuming where we had left off.

"Not really," I said. "I still feel very queasy."

"Well, I guess I better be going," he replied.

"Well I guess!" I nodded, as though he had offered me cash and prizes. I was a lucky girl.

"We didn't get too much rehearsing done," he said, coming up behind me and wrapping his arms around me. "I think maybe we better meet up again sometime this week."

Why, oh why, are the people who are worst at something always the ones who think they are the best? I couldn't wait to send him back out into the danger zone of the rioting city.

The next day I called up my acting teacher and told her I was so sorry I had to leave class because my work schedule had suddenly increased. She sympathized with me, but only offered me a partial refund. I didn't bother to fight. It was more than worth every penny never to see Mr. 90210 again. In his honor, I decided to boycott that entire zip code for the rest of my natural life.

Of course, I went back to obsessing about Carl almost immediately. I guess the bottom line about the flowers was that it was nice of Carl to send them. It's important to give credit where credit is due. A girl certainly always loves to receive a bunch of free flowers. And after all, who really cares what they mean? What does it ever really mean when you send someone flowers? "Thinking of you, but not really thinking too hard."

The other night I had dinner with Janey and Laurel, and we were all talking about how many ways there are to screw up a relationship. It seems like there are almost an infinite number of possibilities. Laurel said, "Why can quantum physics figure out how the smallest particles in the universe should behave in order to make the universe work but no one can figure out how men and women should behave in order to make a relationship work?" I've been thinking how she hit on two areas at once about which I know almost nothing.

So another birthday down the dumper. I feel like I should set some goals for this year. This should be the year that I figure this stuff out. This should be the year where I really identify and then knock off all the bad patterns.

But even more important, from now on I must use my intuition. I must use my ever-growing knowledge of human behavior and all the things I have learned from therapy. When I think I might get involved with someone now I will not sleep with him unless I know for a fact that he loves me. I don't want to be with anyone who is out of touch with his feelings, someone who doesn't want to make a commitment.

And when and if anyone, whoever he might be, decides to send me flowers, I'll just smile and say, "Thank you for the lovely flowers." No big deal. No deep analysis. Just a happy moment because I deserve flowers. I deserve tons of flowers. After all, it really doesn't mean much when someone sends flowers.

I don't plan to respond.

What I Learned This Year:

1. No more fighting with Mom. What is the point of that anyway? I can never win. If I want to beat my head against a wall, with no hope of positive gain, I can go work for human rights or animal rights or women's rights.
2. No more fighting with Dad either. Just let what they both

say roll off me and don't react. Then go home and have some sake.

3. No more ridiculous affairs. Thirty-six years of stupid love is certainly more than enough. No more getting sexual with people I know are totally hopeless.

4. No more voluntary participation in bad sex. Identify it quickly, ignite early warning system, get away. This is the nineties, for God's sake. Not only are the Clintons in the White House, but Hillary is the most impressive first lady we have ever had. Talk about a role model! It's impossible to imagine someone like Hillary Clinton going to bed with a hopeless guy who doesn't give a damn about her feelings and will have sex with just about anyone.

5. No more thinking about Carl. I have had all of those thoughts already.

6. Too bad I didn't grow up in the South. When people from the South look back, seems like they always have such colorful memories. Over and over they meet quirky, fascinating people who share poignant but relevant lessons about the meaning of life. They speak with charming colloquialisms as they wander through the bayous and the swamps. People from the South don't sleep with a guy from an acting class that they took just to get out of the house, a guy so unworthy that he rams their head into the wall behind the bed while the city outside is rioting. No. People from the South recall the smell of magnolia blossoms and the sounds of crickets in the summer heat while they sit with a scruffy but soulful auto mechanic that they used to know in high school. He is playing the harmonica dressed in stressed leather and rolling his own cigarettes. His fingers are yellow from tobacco and black from grease. He has just returned

from working in the oil fields and his eyes contain a painful secret. Maybe it's time for me to start spending more time in the South.

Things I Would Like to Learn in the Coming Year:

1. Something, anything, about quantum physics.
2. More about how the universe works.

Thirty-seven

WELL, THE BIRTHDAY BLUES hit early this year. Right around sunrise in fact.

First thing in the morning, I had to go to my fight-training class, where we practice how to kick a guy in the head and knee a guy in the groin for three and a half hours every Saturday. The whole experience is always alarming, even though the guy in question wears a big padded suit with a big padded head that makes him look a little like one of the lesser Power Rangers.

"Really sock your knee in there," the coach yelled at me today when I didn't use enough force. But today I kept thinking to myself, *It's my fucking birthday. This groin kneeing is as intimate a relationship as I have had with a man in fiscal 1993.* Then I really gave it to the guy. *Take that, Power Ranger!*

In the afternoon, after unbroken decades of receiving presents from Mom that I didn't like—and decades of feeling sad that she wasted time and money on me—as part of my campaign to break my bad patterns I decided to take the bull by the horns and remedy the situation. I asked her if I could accompany her to the store and help pick out my own present.

Everything seemed reasonably pleasant until the moment we actually walked in the door of Saks Fifth Avenue and began examining entire racks of clothes like representatives of two entirely different cultures.

Mom began holding up outfit after outfit for me to consider, never even accidentally stumbling onto anything I could imagine myself wearing.

"Isn't this adorable?" she would say, waving a synthetic two-piece royal blue knit suit with a gathered waist and gold braided trim.

"Uh, yes, it's great, Mom," I'd mumble, afraid to say anything too negative, growing increasingly anxious watching her face collapse into her grimmest expression. "But I don't really have anyplace to wear an outfit like that."

"You don't need a special place to wear an outfit like this. It's perfect for anything you might have to do in the course of a day. You just don't like anything nice," she replied, exhaling enough carbon dioxide to suffocate every living thing in the Juniors department.

I was transported back to dozens of other shopping occasions almost exactly like this one during which my opinions always seemed to be an embarrassment and a burden to my mother. With each passing moment the mood between us would grow bigger and darker until it felt like all the air had been sucked out of the store. I would start to imagine myself curled into a ball on the floor of a dressing room as mountains of clothes on hangers were piled on top of me.

"Mom, you know what I'd really like for my birthday?" I

said, trying to infuse my voice with so much good-natured enthusiasm it would change her outlook on everything. "I could really use a white jacket."

"Hmmmph," she grunted.

I took a couple of white jackets over to a mirror to try them on. The very first one struck me as so flattering, I felt a little giddy at the thought that I might score a birthday present I genuinely liked!

I began thinking to myself, *If I just take this now, and we blow out of here immediately, maybe we can avoid the fight that appears to be looming on the horizon like a high-pressure weather system.*

I looked up at my mother, who now resembled someone making the long slow walk to the gallows. She sighed and shook her head a silent rolling no as she followed me to the cashier. I had interpreted her expression correctly. I had ruined her life.

"This is the last time I go along with one of your stupid ideas," she said. "I get absolutely no pleasure buying you a gift that I don't happen to like."

I almost ran across the room to retrieve the blue suit with the gold buttons as a gesture of reconciliation, but decided to hold my ground. My mother was white with rage.

I guess it was the dumb girl in me who was thinking there could be a sane solution to a problem with my mother. She continued to make it very clear that she would never tolerate any solution initiated by me. Even now that I was thirty-seven. Especially now that I went and ruined her enjoyment of my birthday. I hope I'm very happy. Me and my highfalutin ideas.

Eventually we went to meet my father for the big Birthday Dinner.

"How'd you girls do?" he said, grinning.

"Don't even ask," she said. "It was a complete disaster."

"So!" I said, trying to change the mood. "What have you two been up to lately? How are the physical ailments of your friends and relatives and all their children I have never met?"

I didn't actually want the answer to this question. I wanted to talk about the art lesson I taught that day where I had everyone in the class draw an outline of their torso and then where their heart was supposed to be. I had them do a magazine collage of all the things in them that were broken. The results were very touching. Miguel cut up a picture of the girl who dumped him, then divvied it up like a jigsaw puzzle. Christian put in a sliced-up photo of his father, who took off ten years ago without telling anyone. But I didn't want to give my parents a chance to pick apart something that I felt good about. I also knew that the defects and tragedies of the people in my mother's life was a topic that always seemed to buoy her. I wanted something really distracting to take the attention off of the afternoon's birthday present debacle.

"I don't think she's heard about Justine," my father said. Justine was one name I would have never brought up. My mother's friend Justine was a very odd duck. She was a good match for my mother as they were two imperious peas in a pod. They both liked to pepper their speech with embarrassing French phrases. Both said *"Du café?"* when they offered coffee. Both referred to an apartment as a pied-à-terre.

Both readily tossed *"Je ne sais quoi"* and *"Qu'est-ce que c'est?"* and *"Mon Dieu!"* into ordinary conversation as often as possible.

My mother admired, even worshipped, Justine. She spoke often about Justine's great beauty and fashion expertise even though Justine was the horsiest-faced woman I'd ever met. According to my mother, Justine once had a career as a model. "A model *what*?" is the question I always wanted to ask.

But as my mother saw it, Justine was an authority on appearance. "You should wear your hair straight back off your face," she always said to me, pulling my hair back in a way that made me appear to have male-pattern baldness. Justine was very fond of velveteen hair accents, bold-patterned scarves, and short, boxy sweaters that made even slim women look thick waisted.

My mother's main obsession with Justine centered around what she believed to be Justine's giant crush on my father. "You are so lucky to have such a fantastic guy," Justine supposedly always said. "He is a gift from the Heavens."

At the top of her list of my father's God-given heavenly gifts was what she saw as his astonishing self-reliance.

"Just the way he gets up in the morning and makes his own breakfast," she would sigh. "I have to cook something every single morning for Jack."

She was referring to the fact that my father not only knew how to pour himself a bowl of Bran Flakes and a six-ounce glass of orange juice, totally unassisted, but could also duplicate the photo on the back of the cereal box by making himself a piece of toast, cut on the diagonal, topped with a rectangle of butter. Justine could easily stretch the process of oohing and aahing at my father's ability to make his own cold cereal tableau into a full half hour.

"What happened to Justine?" I asked. I saw my mother's expression begin to collapse. I knew I had asked the wrong question. She began to dab at her eyes with a Kleenex. And then, preparing for a full meltdown, she put her sunglasses on.

"You tell her," said my mother. "I can't talk about it."

"She killed herself," my father said. "They found her sitting on her sunporch with a dry-cleaning bag over her head."

I knew this was horrible, but something about the melodrama of the moment and the image of the dry-cleaning bag hit me as funny. I started imagining Justine, sandwiched inside the long, clear plastic bag with hanger handles coming out of the top above her hair. I saw her sitting upright, hands folded, in between nicely pressed skirts and blouses enveloped in crisp new tissue paper.

A laugh started to escape. I quickly transformed it into a gasp, then a cough.

The only reason it didn't draw more attention was because my mother was in her glory, dominating my birthday from a throne of tragedy. When the waiter brought the birthday champagne, he hesitated momentarily, wondering if this was the right table.

Lucky for me, my mother was too choked up on her own melodrama to offer her traditional nerve-racking toast.

On the bright side, the dismal details of Justine's death became the focus of my birthday festivities, instead of the usual fights with the restaurant employees. So riveting were they to my mother, and so comfortable was she in the grand drama of her grief, that the kitchen help and I both gathered on some other plane in another dimension, to cheer, throw handfuls of confetti, and slap each other on the back.

But the fun was only beginning. After dinner, we pulled into my driveway just in time to see a florist delivery truck dropping something off on my front steps. My pulse quickened. Not the flowers from Carl again! Two entire years after our breakup, one ill-timed week after I had finally purged my house of every item he had left behind—including old shirts of his that I used to sleep in and the few clothes of his still hanging in the closet that I had for some reason left around because they gave me a vague feeling of comfort.

I had finally thrown out all of the household items that he had too much of a hand in selecting. When we lived together, he had the final word on every single purchase. Every lamp I bought without his approval had to be taken back and exchanged. Every choice I made without consultation was questioned. Everything in the house—sheets, towels, upholstery, carpet—was charcoal gray, his favorite color.

But it finally occurred to me that if I could stand all the shopping and the driving, I could now change everything. I had never structured a household around my own preferences before. I wasn't even sure what my own preferences were.

I became so excited by the idea of all the possibilities that I bought a towel, bath mat, and washcloth in every bright color they made. I also bought one of every color of dish towel, coffee mug, pot holder, and plate. It was a veritable rainbow of boring household items.

Maybe it was kind of a stupid thing to do but I was so thrilled that now there was no one around to complain no matter what I did. As long as I remembered to keep the closet doors closed when my mother visited, I was home free!

I'd finally stumbled onto the pleasurable side of the breakup: the total cessation of group decisions. One great thing I noticed about living all by myself: All of my annoying habits seemed to have disappeared.

I got an awful lot of pleasure out of throwing all those gray towels and mugs in the Salvation Army bin. It felt like getting on a scale and noticing that I had suddenly lost five pounds. It inspired me to go through my closet and throw out everything else I associated too closely with Carl.

Like the lingerie I bought after reading advice in a woman's magazine about how to revive a lackluster love life. It was a kind of a lacy snap-under-the-crotch Victoria's Secret one-piece that had a see-through thing that you wore on top if you wanted. One painful afternoon, after working out for weeks to build my confidence, I decided to put it on and surprise him. I would just be wearing it, seductively, when he walked in the door. I wasn't sure what activity besides sex went with lingerie. Window washing seemed a little risky. So I opted for trying to look sexy while cooking dinner. He would find me so irresistible that dinner would have to wait. The magazine practically guaranteed it.

My heart was pounding when I heard him put his key in the lock.

"Do I smell sausages?" he said.

"Yes," I replied.

"Why are you making sausages?" he asked, coming into the kitchen.

"I'm putting sausages in the pasta sauce," I told him.

"Oh," he said, as he picked up his mail and headed for the back bedroom. I heard him boot up the computer. And that's where he sat until I said dinner was ready.

Meanwhile, I retreated into the bedroom and changed back into jeans and a T-shirt.

"How come you were wearing that thing you had on when I came in?" he eventually asked, with a mouth full of sausage.

"I don't know," I said, deciding never to expect anything from him ever again.

But now here were at least a hundred dollars' worth of flowers and that same card as last year: "Happy Birthday Carl." Just like they were for him again. But now even more mysterious in terms of possible motives.

A gigantic arrangement of mostly yellow flowers. About a dozen yellow tulips, and a dozen yellow roses, with a few lilacs and hyacinths around the edges for accents. It looked kind of cryptic, as though all that yellow was supposed to mean something. But what? Fear? Was he feeling afraid? Afraid of what? Afraid of losing touch?

And, damn it, once again I could feel the tears welling up in my eyes. Was I pretending the flowers carried a message of regret? Was the dumb girl in me trying to convince me that they contained a wordless apology?

"Completely empty gesture" is what my friend Laurel said, giving me a book to read about Maria Callas, longtime lover of Aristotle Onassis. Apparently on the day he betrayed her by marrying Jacqueline Kennedy, he had helicopters fly over Callas's island home and drop hundreds and hundreds of roses. "A perfect example of an empty gesture," Laurel said, rolling her eyes. "It means absolutely nothing. Here he's in the middle of marrying Jackie Kennedy and he still has to guilt-jerk poor Maria Callas within an inch of her life."

I guess I wouldn't be spending so much time fretting about this again if I had something else to absorb my attention. Talk about a year that was unproductive romantically—even its best moments came in well under the radar. It seems wrong to mention Mumbling Boy in this context. Although I do feel he deserves some sort of a mention. He was the bartender who decided to hit on me at the big art opening they had for Michael, of James and Michael (from the art department at my school). In attendance were *all* of the And-Michaels (Dawn and Michael, Candace and Michael, and of course James and Michael). And me: the only single person in our group, as well as the only person without a Michael. So when the okay-looking bartender came over and sat down beside me, for a minute I was hopeful and flattered. That was before I realized I couldn't understand a single word out of his mouth. He barely moved his lips, as though he were doing ventriloquism without a dummy.

"Mmmble bmmph mmmph bmble," he would say.

"Huh! Great!" I would reply.

I made a brief initial attempt to get him to repeat things more clearly, but even when he repeated them, it was like he was speaking during dental surgery with a mouth full of cotton wadding. It seemed kind of rude to keep asking him to repeat himself, so I settled into a pattern of head-nodding and agreeable face-making. "Grm nmnph mmph blmbmph," he'd offer.

"Oh! No kidding!" I'd nod. "Interesting!"

And I kept that up until something he said jumped out at me. Was I crazy or had he just asked me if I had a bikini wax? That's when I realized that he had invited me to go on a road trip to Mexico with him after the party. *"¡Las señoritas muy bonitas!"* he said, snapping his fingers and swaying to a mariachi cliché that was playing in his head, which is also when it hit me that I had virtually no idea at all what I had been nodding yes to for the previous half hour. Had I agreed to help him knock over a gas station? Had I said I'd like to join his stable of hos? I looked down at my wristwatch feigning great surprise, gasped loudly, and explained that I had to get home right away. As I left, Mumble Boy sat, watching me exit, making flamboyant gestures to all the And-Michaels to indicate that he thought I was insane.

And that is pretty much typical of the romance that was fiscal 1993. Except, I suppose, that this was also the year of Clay Zimler.

Last year on my birthday I resolved not to get involved with anyone who didn't love me. That's how Clay slipped in unnoticed. He seemed to love me almost from the first moment. When I was introduced to Clay at Joan-from-the-English-department's big birthday party, he started flirting with me in such a practiced way that my intuition told me to turn and run. He was too handsome, too slick, too charming. But when I confessed this to Laurel, she gave me so much shit that I backed off my own instincts. The more I thought about it, the more I realized she was right. How crazy was I to hold someone's good looks against him? Wasn't that like rejecting a person because he wasn't a loser? So I flirted back.

I ended up going to dinner with him a few days later at one of those whacked-out Italian places where they have Christmas lights and taxidermied animal heads and hundred-gallon jars of stuffed olives and peppers that always make me wonder if the stuff inside could be eaten in the event of a nuclear attack or if even then they'd be too disgusting.

Right from those first moments in the restaurant, it was like Clay was taking care of me. He ordered wine and appetizers, he knew the waiters, he recommended what I should have for dinner and even ordered for me. He was smart and funny and interesting and an okay makeout. And he *really* seemed to like me an awful lot. Which frankly kind of scared me because he was coming toward me like a speeding train. He seemed to be so crazy about me so soon that it didn't make any sense to me.

Which, of course, was when Laurel let me have it with both barrels. "You are letting your goddamn low self-esteem hold you emotional hostage," she said. "Someone liking you is a *good* thing, not a *danger* sign. You really should start seeing your shrink again."

I figured she was right. I was definitely searching for early warning signs like a patient recovering from a terminal illness. It was becoming second nature for me to do so. If he was as pulled together as he appeared, why the chain-smoking? He was the most aggressive smoker I had ever met. He had the amazing ability to chew his food and keep a lit cigarette dangling intact on the edge of his lip, undisturbed by vigorous mastication. Even while eating spareribs, corn on the cob, or soup, in a nonsmoking environment, he smoked so much that you could bake by his smoking breaks. He would step outside every fifteen minutes to hulk in front of a doorway. If you put chocolate chip cookies into the oven when he first lit up, they'd be moist, chewy, and a delightful golden brown by the next time he had to step outside.

Then there was the cryptic comment from the friend of his we ran into at the restaurant, who came over to me and whispered, "This is so good for him to have a girlfriend in the same city. Usually he dates people who live on another coast if not another continent entirely."

I knew I needed to decode this message, but I just didn't have the equipment.

And then there was the pager that he carried in the back pocket of his pants. On our first date, it beeped continually. He would take it out and look at it many times an hour, then excuse himself and go to a pay phone to return calls.

By about the fifth call, when he hadn't volunteered any information, I asked him who was paging. "Some of it is business, some of it is personal" is all he said. It felt impolite to probe further.

On our second date I was thrown into a complete tizzy when he kissed me very gently and said, "I am so in love with you. I have never felt like this about anyone before." Even as I stared into his face, which was beaming with sincerity, my brain was racing. *How can you love me?* it was saying. *You have only known me a couple of days.*

When I expressed these concerns to Laurel, of course she went nuts again. I was intentionally trying to sabotage my first new chance at love. Ever since the breakup with Carl I had gotten too comfortable being miserable, she said. I needed to talk to the shrink about why I couldn't relax and enjoy this wonderful new chapter in my life.

Once again it seemed like she was right. What was wrong with me anyway? Here I had acquired Mr. Wonderful and I was scanning the territory for land mines. My refusal to believe that I was worthy of love was causing me to cast aspersions randomly and for no reason.

That weekend I came down with some kind of flu or cold thing and canceled a dinner we had planned. I was going to lie low till it blew over. When I got sick around Carl, he would always make a point of letting me know how inconvenienced he was by it.

Which is why I was so surprised when the next thing I knew Clay was in my kitchen making me soup and hot rolls. Yes, he put so much pepper in the soup that it was inedible. (Lucky for me, my illness allowed me to eat only a few spoonfuls.) But it was the kindness of the gesture that really got to me.

No one had ever exhibited such good-natured interest in taking care of me before. Not even my own mother.

"You're amazing," I said to him. "I don't know why you're working this hard."

"Because I just feel so lucky that we found each other when we did," he said to me.

Then he sat with me and we watched TV together for hours, which otherwise would have been an ordeal since all they were showing was those Waco, Texas–Branch Davidian–FBI hostage updates. It was hard to find a station that wasn't airing bulletins about "Day 38" of the big standoff featuring reporters with nothing at all to say who were nonetheless so excited about getting camera time that they would just say something at length anyway.

"That's how real unconditional love works," I started to lecture myself, when I would begin to worry about our relationship. "I have lived a life of such serious deprivation that I'm like a starving person at an all-you-can-eat buffet." I tried to ignore the nervous voice in my head that kept repeating, *What did I do to make him love me so damn much this soon?* and *If he loves me so much, why haven't we slept together yet?*

To calm myself down, I bought a book from the sale bin at Borders called *The Way That We Met*. In it, all these longtime married couples talked about how they were first thrown together in a wide variety of unexpected encounters: at parties, at bus stops, in doctors' reception rooms. The thing that was striking was how in every case they claimed to know immediately. Something somewhere deep inside of all of them told them this was the one.

That was my whole problem, I decided. I was so armored against pain that I wasn't open or vulnerable enough to hear my something-somewhere-deep-inside voice. Clay was more un-spoiled than I was. He was still in touch with his something-somewhere-deep-inside. Mine was pitifully blocked.

The whole key to finding real love and happiness in this world, I decided, was to just shut up and interact with the something-somewhere-deep-inside people. They were the human equivalents of geese who knew the first time out how to fly south for the winter. I was lucky to have met someone who was so much more in tune with reality than I was.

We were supposed to get together the following Saturday night. I hadn't seen Clay all week, although I had spoken with him almost every evening. He always called about five o'clock. I was never exactly prepared when this very intimate voice would want to know, "How was your day?"

"I miss you," he would say to me. "I wish I could be there with you."

"Well, why don't you come on over?" I'd say. But he never could. More than once I wondered if this was the strategy of a very smart man who had learned that absence makes the heart grow fonder. Or the strategy of a very busy man. Or a very lazy man. Or a man with a very, very big secret.

I didn't let it bother me because all the tension that was building between us was promising to turn the weekend into something amazing. I was so hot for him that I felt like if you put popcorn kernels anywhere on my body they would pop.

Saturday was our one-month anniversary. We still hadn't slept together. He was waiting until it was really right, I told myself. He would know. That something-somewhere-deep-inside would cue him. Meanwhile he wanted to cook a special dinner for me, he said. Then he showed up with a brand-new hibachi and tongs and an apron and two bags of groceries.

He was magnificent. He told jokes as he made his own marinade with fresh tomatoes and lemons and shallots and red wine. Like other guys I knew who cooked, he had some unusual cooking ideas. But I didn't so much as raise an eyebrow for fear of putting a damper on his enthusiasm when he added radishes and cucumbers to the spaghetti sauce. I just looked on admiringly.

He actually set the table. He brought flowers and a big bulky aromatherapy candle that smelled like the back room at a New Age bookstore. He also bought a bottle of wine. (Yes, it tasted exactly like Sprite . . . but it was the thought that counted.)

Every effort he made was very touching. That he cared enough to bother doing anything was more than I was used to. I could never have counted on Carl to do something when it was called for, because it brought out a contrarian streak in him that pretty much ensured he'd do nothing.

So as I sat beaming by the big plate of leathery barbecued fish and rubbery broccoli that Clay had labored over, I felt my eyes welling up with tears. Before I knew what I had done, I told him that I loved him, too. He smiled shyly.

That was when I talked him into spending the night. This time, when he didn't argue or resist, I thought I might swoon. All this waiting to have sex had made me so incredibly ready.

But from the moment the clothes were off, every movement between us was awkward. More alarmingly, his touch was cold. His kissing was suddenly dispassionate and remote, like his lips had gone dead.

I, of course, went ahead and acted really, really, really turned on. Maybe, I thought, some polar opposite behavior could counter and neutralize his. Maybe it was just me, I thought. Who knew? After all, there were only two of us there.

Which was why I pretended not to notice when he took a smoking break fifteen minutes into the middle of what was passing for foreplay. (And what was passing for foreplay was so miscalculated it would probably have been much more accurately labeled threeplay.)

I had decided not to care. Things would definitely get better with time, I said to myself. How could they not? So he had some sexual issues. So what? As long as he loved me, I could wait until he felt more comfortable. There was no stopping real love. Especially since Clay was a guy whose something-somewhere-deep-inside voice knew we should be together. Comfort and ease were inevitable if I was patient. And I could be patient. Obviously I could wait.

Meanwhile I'd be the most supportive person that he'd ever met. I would show him he hadn't been wrong to have such deep feelings for me. Which is why, in the interest of our wonderful future together, I faked the biggest orgasm I have ever faked. It was a full 75 percent bigger than my last really big fake-out. I was prepared to pull out all the stops and fake multiples, but the whole event didn't last long enough for that.

That night he got up four different times to stand in the kitchen and smoke. At two, at three-thirty, at five, and again at six-fifteen. I pretended to be asleep. By seven he was dressed and gone without even saying a word.

The following week he was kind of hard to find. He explained that he had some kind of stomach problem. Maybe he was coming down with something, he thought. So I immediately sprang into action. I would take care of him.

He was having none of it.

I decided he was being a martyr. So despite his protestations, I went ahead and made a pot of homemade soup to bring over to his apartment. Even though it was only the second pot of soup that I had ever made, I figured no way could it be as awful as that peppery nightmare he'd concocted. I picked out a Betty Crocker recipe from a book so unused that I had to cut the plastic cover off. I felt that Betty Crocker probably knew something about pleasing a reluctant man. I also desperately wanted to see where he lived.

When he met me at the door, in his bathrobe, it was clear by his expression that he did not want me to come inside. He seemed happy enough to receive the free soup but also made it clear that he wanted to be alone. He stood blocking the entrance, making no move to invite me in.

I could see, over his shoulder, that the apartment was tiny—just two rooms. It was the kind of crash pad that a guy in his early twenties would inhabit, not a thirtysomething financial counselor. There were sheets hanging on the windows, no real furniture to speak of, and several dead plants in inappropriately fancy festive pots. *Presents from girlfriends who didn't last long enough to come by and water them* is what I was thinking.

I asked him if I could use the bathroom, knowing he couldn't really say no. Which is how I learned that he used the shower-curtain rod as a place to hang his suits in lieu of the closet. The surface of the shower itself was a petri dish of mold and bacteria. If the relationship progressed, I would definitely need to get a tetanus booster before I spent the night.

On my way back to the front door, I couldn't help but notice a bunch of snapshots of different twentysomething females
in various poses in picture-frame magnets on the front of the
refrigerator. Kind of like a *Playboy* spread: Clay's Girls of Re-
frigeration. But I was too self-conscious from his anxiety at
my presence to stop and scrutinize them. He was watching me
like a department store detective on the lookout for teenage
shoplifters.

On the drive home, I decided to wait until he felt better before I asked the hard questions. Meanwhile he continued calling every night. His phone conversations were still full of "I
miss you" and "I wish we could be together." But he never offered to actually make the drive to come and see me.

I waited a few more days. Then I decided I had to confront
him. I thought about what I would say for a full day before I
said it, like it was my move next in a really odd game of chess.
If I said the right thing, I might revive our decaying energy.
But if my phrasing was off, I would lose the match altogether.

It seemed that I could gain the maximum advantage if I led
with affection, so "I need to see you. I miss you" was how I
opened. No arguing with that, I thought. No way to misinter-
pret it or be insulted by it. It was really a compliment.

"I feel the same way," he said, "but my schedule has gotten
completely crazy." He was "incredibly busy," he said. No arguing with that either.

The following week Mom had to go into the hospital to
have polyps removed. She had been suffering with intestinal
ailments for the past thirty years. To me, they always seemed
like a by-product of her never-ending anger and tension, but of
course I couldn't say that to her.

I went to stay at their house to help Dad out with whatever. And as I sat quietly in what was once my bedroom, sinking into a morass of stress and boredom, drinking a giant tumbler of gin that I sneaked from Dad's liquor cabinet while he was watching *NYPD Blue* (just the way I used to when I was back in high school, only then it used to be during *The Rockford Files*), Clay phoned.

"I think it is time for us to stop seeing each other," he said.

I was silent.

"I feel like you want more from me than I know how to give. Nothing I do ever seems like enough for you," he said, as the sound of a million buzzing bees filled my brain. "I feel eaten alive. I can't take it anymore."

I could hear him smoking all the way through the call.

I congratulated him on his timing. At some point I hung up. But in that moment, in a blinding flash, I decoded what his friend had said about never dating women in the same city. He preferred women who lived great geographical distances away because they made his need to be alone seem like thwarted desire. He could yearn for a relationship without having to participate in one. He had been treating me like I lived in another city. Our problem was I just lived too nearby.

Three months total, from introduction to I love you to the worst-timed breakup in my history, with a few lovely and not inexpensive parting gifts thrown in for what seems like in retrospect no reason at all.

The first thing I thought about was how he had said, "I love you more than anyone else I have ever known," more than anyone else I have ever known. Maybe what he really meant was "I think I am having an actual feeling."

Of course Laurel had a book to explain away this one, too. "They totally nail his ass in *Men Who Can't Love,* she said giddily. "He's the most perfect specimen of that whole premise ever. It's about guys who are emotionally eaten alive by their frustrated, unhappy mothers who expect them to act in husbandlike ways because their real husbands are absent or too fed up to play along anymore. The guys know this is warped. They know they can never be a husband to their mothers. So they come to the conclusion that since it's impossible to ever give Mommy what she wants, it's impossible to please any woman period. The only time these guys are truly comfortable is when a relationship is just beginning, because then there is pursuit but no commitment. Or at the very end. The middle part—the part that would contain the relationship—makes them feel like they're being suffocated.

"He fits the checklist in the book down to every detail," she said, proudly. Meanwhile I'd already wasted three confusing months plus the month-and-a-half recovery period, following the formula that it takes half the time the relationship lasted to recover from it. How many of these symptom-specific checklists was I supposed to know by heart before I got involved with a guy?

Which brings me back to this year's giant yellow tulip and rose assortment. This year they really did seem like a message in code.

I sat down at the computer and punched combinations of words into a search engine until I found a couple of guides to the symbolism of flowers. According to one elaborate florist's dictionary, yellow tulips meant "False hopes. You never cared for me anyway."

Stranger still, yellow roses meant "I am jealous of you." Jealous? Jealous of *what*? Could he really have spent all that money on flowers just for the chance to be whiny and unpleasant in a way that required research to understand?

Then I noticed an additional detail: the accent flowers. According to the same dictionary, lilacs meant "You have awoken my heart again." Even more amazing, hyacinths meant "I regret our unfortunate breakup."

So was he saying that although for the most part he still felt awful and envious, he also had regrets? Was there any chance in hell that he was aware of these meanings? Or was trying to read meanings into flower choices like trying to tell the future by examining the intestines of a chicken?

Why is my life always full of people who have elaborate ways not to say anything that I can understand.

Happy Birthday to me.

What I Learned This Year That I Need to Remember:

1. I have to trust my instincts. When I have started to lecture myself in order to bypass them is when I know I need to worry.
2. It's ridiculous to always assume my friends know more about what is going on than I do, just because they have read a bunch of pop psychology. I love my friends, but it may be because they are as fucked up as I am.
3. Be wary of men who love too much too soon for no reason.
4. No more faking orgasms to help an inept guy have better self-esteem than I am exhibiting by faking orgasms in the first place.
5. No more shopping with Mom. No more trying to manipu-

late any situation with her, period. Whatever she wants to do is fine. Say nothing. Detach. Live through it smiling. Then go home and drink sake until the urge to say something to her has passed.

What I Would Like to Learn in the Coming Year:

1. More about how the universe works. I know I said this last year. And I did try. I bought that book by Stephen Hawking about the big bang and black holes. I planned to read it, underline it, take notes and test myself. But I only got as far as the first page, which I read at least two hundred times, always falling asleep on the same sentence in the middle of the first paragraph of page two. To say that this year I would like to do a lot better is to insult myself. I can't set the bar that low.
2. Something, anything, about quantum physics.

Thirty-Fucking-Eight

WELL, THE YEAR STARTED with a very clear message.

No more saying "Sure, why not?" to almost strangers who offer to fix me up with guys they "think I'll like." Case in point, the big Super Bowl party, exactly a year ago. A woman I met at the gym (Kelly, the one who never seems to get off the treadmill) said she had a guy friend she wanted me to meet. That the only thing I knew about Kelly was how much I envied her biceps made me think the odds that she would have any idea what I might like were not with me. But I decided to play along, thus dispensing with my annual Super Bowl tradition of trying not to hear even one single second of the game.

By the time I arrived at Kelly's house in Studio City, the television was blaring. Most of the males in attendance, a real mixed bag of jock goons in backward baseball caps and team shirts, were gathered around the TV. Kelly and a couple of her female friends who I vaguely recognized from the gym (Exercycle Woman *and* The-woman-who-lies-on-the-giant-green-ball, both dressed in tight tank tops that showed off their tanned glistening breasts) were hanging out in the kitchen, by the buffet, picking at the icing on the cake, breaking off small pieces of the turkey, searching for cashews in the Chinese chicken salad. And drinking. They were really drinking. Kelly was as drunk as anyone I have ever seen. She was gulping red wine by the ten-ounce tumbler. I remember thinking that even though her eyes were glazed, her thighs and her biceps still looked very impressive. She was a good advertisement for alcoholism as a valuable aid to muscle tone.

Immediately she pulled me by the arm into the group of men glued to the Super Bowl broadcast and introduced me to a pleasant-looking guy in an army jacket. I don't know what my reaction was to him. I really didn't get any vibes. He wasn't notably good- or bad-looking, immediately intriguing, or particularly repulsive. We only got as far as hello. Whatever small talk we might have made was instantly drowned out by the cheering football fans on all sides of us. It was clear that fix-up boy really wanted to be watching the game instead of meeting me at this particular moment. And since feeling like an inconvenience is not particularly erotic, I waved and made a facial expression I hoped he would interpret as "Talk to you later." Then I headed into the kitchen to pick at icing and look for cashews with the girls. I figured if anything was to develop, after the game would be a better time.

I was making myself a turkey sandwich when Kelly caught up with me again, grabbed me by the arm, and started talking in that shockingly loud voice that only a drunk or a totally deaf person would ever use.

"What do you think of him?" is how she began. She was literally *shouting*.

Immediately embarrassed, I turned to see if he was looking. It seemed to me that he was because he looked away really fast. The kitchen was only a few feet from the group that was watching the game. "I think he really likes you," Kelly screamed at me. Why she interpreted his fixation on the Super Bowl as early sparks of love was a question I forgot to ask. Mainly I was overwhelmed with humiliation that he might be able to hear us.

This time I was too frozen with terror to turn and see his reaction. I attempted to "shhh" her but she was so loaded she couldn't comprehend the concept of anxiety. So I picked up my plate of food and tried to back her into a corner of the apartment where her voice could not be heard. But the apartment was not that big. There was no such place.

"He has a really big dick," she shouted, as I tried to figure out how to dissolve molecularly and reassemble in another part of town. "I know that for a fact because I fucked him! He's a really good fuck," she screamed.

Oh good, I thought. *Perfect. Just what I hoped for. A chance to meet a new man just a few seconds before I am forced to kill myself.* "It didn't work out with us," she continued at full volume, "but I think he really likes you! Do you like him? He has the biggest dick I've ever seen."

This left me with only one option as I saw it: finding the quickest route to the door. By the time I exited, Kelly was lying facedown on the floor in the living room, in front of the television set, out cold and snoring loudly. The drool that was leaking out of her mouth was creating a wet spot on the carpet. All around her, a room full of Super Bowl fans kept rooting for whoever. No one said a thing. No one seemed to notice. Not even the guy with the really big dick.

Anyway, I decided right then: No more fix-ups by people I don't even know. Never again. Never ever.

A couple of weeks later Mom's childhood friend Evelyn came out to stay with them for ten days. Almost immediately, Mom got fixated on the thought that Evelyn was "interested in Dad." Yet another woman presumably dazzled by his incredible cereal-preparation ability.

I don't want to put Dad down. He may have his charms, although in my opinion he keeps them very well hidden. At sixty-eight, he is forty pounds overweight and the owner of three chins. Evelyn, on the other hand, always looked cute and fit in a sixtysomething way, all dressed up in her hunter green jacket with the leopard-skin trim, matching hat, belt, gloves, and three-inch heels.

By the time she departed, Mom would end her portion of every marital argument with "Fine. Well, maybe things will be better when you're with Evelyn."

I did notice that Evelyn had a remarkable capacity for dealing with Dad's habit of explaining simple concepts as though she had never heard of them before. She seemed to have as much good-natured patience for this as my mother. I watched her listen to a dissertation on how she might better hold her fork and knife while she ate, as if she hadn't been living a life full of fork and knife holding for over six decades. She actually smiled as if she was grateful for the tips.

Before I saw that with my own eyes, I often wondered, *How many women besides my mother could stand to listen to a list of instructions on how to put a CD back in its case many hundreds of times? Who, besides her, could sit still for directions on how to refold a map?* I considered him incredibly lucky to have found the one woman who could deal with this behavior without strangling him. Now watching Evelyn take it all without flinching made me think maybe I didn't really know what the hell was going on with women of that generation. Or maybe my mother was right. Maybe Evelyn had ulterior motives.

Evelyn always struck me as the sanest one of my mother's peers, not that I was sure if such a category existed. So one afternoon during her visit, while my mother was at the doctor having yet another set of tests for another set of ailments, I decided to take Evelyn to lunch and scope out her motives for myself.

As I watched her eat the biggest bowl of pasta with clams I have ever seen a small, aging woman consume at one sitting, she waxed nostalgic about her long wonderful years of wedded bliss to the deceased and incredibly obese narcissist, Fred. Awestruck by such longevity in a marriage, especially to a huge, fat guy, I asked her, "What was the secret to your success as a couple?"

"Well, dear," she said, sipping a glass of white wine, "the key was that he was a wonderful man. You have to start with that. But as I'm sure you know, marriage is far from easy. There wasn't a day that went by when he didn't make me cry."

"Then how can you call that a happy marriage?" I gasped. "How can you call him a wonderful man if he made you cry every day?"

"It wasn't *all* day every day," she replied, carefully buttering a hot roll. "Sweetheart, in marriage you learn to take the good with the bad."

Words to live by, since this year might have been my lamest birthday to date.

Every year before the folks come over I begin to compulsively clean my house and arrange my person to the sound of a permanent tape of my mother's derisive voice playing in my head, pointing out all my millions and millions of inadequacies. Then I try to follow the trail of her complaints, like Hansel and Gretel with their bread crumbs, toward her version of perfection.

One year as sort of a joke, I went around to all the teachers at the after-school faculty meeting about an hour before the big birthday dinner. "Really look at me critically," I said to them all, "because something is very wrong with me. As soon as I walk into the room, my mother will point it out." I was wearing a brand-new outfit and new shoes. I had had my hair washed and blow-dried at a salon during lunch break. No one at work could spot anything wrong (although one of my students thought my skirt was "so eighties").

So just for the sport of it, and as a measure of my own growth, this year I decided to see if I could second-guess my mother by predicting my own flaws. As I carefully recalled my critiques from previous years, I saw that her complaints fell into certain predictable patterns. The most popular were weight ("Have you put on weight?" or "You look practically anorexic"), hair length and style ("What kind of a hairstyle is that? It looks like you've been cutting your own hair," or "Your hair is much too thin to handle that kind of cut"), makeup amount and technique ("So, have you given up on wearing makeup altogether? Isn't being attractive important to you anymore?" or "You should go down to Saks Fifth Avenue and talk to a makeup professional. Where would you get the idea that so much eye shadow is flattering?"). Clothes could present a wide variety of problems by being too old ("Why don't you throw out that disgusting thing already?") or too trendy ("Aren't you a little old to be dressing like a teenager?"). They could be too tight ("What size skirt is that? Whatever it is, I think you could have used the next size up") or too loose-fitting ("That sweater was clearly designed for someone with a bigger bustline. You just don't fill it out"). They could also be wrong for the season ("I just don't understand why you would wear something made out of T-shirt material in the middle of winter"). There was a lot of discussion about being dressed too warmly or not warmly enough, about needing more sweaters or coats, or fewer. It was anyone's guess which of these things would be circled on her checklist. The only certainty was that it would be some of them.

I decided to go with 1) Hair too long, not sufficiently styled, and 2) Clothes somehow poorly maintained.

Then I had the carpets shampooed and the windows professionally washed. It was my goal, and an interesting challenge, to see if I could achieve a birthday where we moved as quickly as possible past the topic of my shortcomings to the always more pleasing topic of the shortcomings of others.

Since Mom had been sick recently, I made a special effort to do everything in my power to be ready to neutralize any assault.

Toward this end, I scheduled an emergency meeting with the shrink on the morning of my birthday to show me how to troubleshoot likely situations before bullets began to fly.

"The afternoon always starts out friendly," I explained. "It's like she throws that in as a decoy to remind me that a positive emotional connection is still a possibility if I play my cards right. But then she starts to pick fights as soon as the greeting period dies down, as soon as she starts to get too comfortable. It's almost like she's bored. Sometimes I think she isn't interested in her own life except when she is picking a fight."

"Don't let her engage you" is what the shrink offered. "Lay back. Become laconic. Perhaps say something like 'Mom, you seem to be in a very bad mood. Why don't we talk again when you're feeling better?'"

Perfect, I thought to myself, *for when we vacation on Neptune.* On this planet I could never *ever* say a thing like that to my mother. That would amount to adding so much oil to the fire that I'd better be wearing an asbestos suit and carrying marshmallows.

I even tried to talk to Dad about it. Of course he refused to believe that she ever had anything to do with provoking the fights.

"That's ridiculous" is what he said to me. "Your mother would never intentionally pick a fight with you. You've always been overly sensitive."

In my father's worldview, he and my mother were only guilty of the best intentions, of loving too deeply and too well. Their message was that anyone who truly loved me had an obligation to tell me how far off the mark I was whenever they could.

Perhaps the greatest indicator of how hard I was trying this year was the fact that I actually turned on a vacuum cleaner during televised O.J. trial analysis. That trial, and every additional moment of O.J.-related programming, was the only television I really watched. I internalized its details to such an extent that I walked around all day long thinking about hair and fiber analysis and DNA, constantly listening to the voices of Marcia Clark and Johnnie Cochran in my head, interrogating me as I went about my business. "What did you do after you finished vacuuming?" I would hear one of them ask, as if somehow my schedule was relevant to the outcome of the trial.

"Oh? And then after you took out the garbage what did you do?" One day I cut my finger with a knife while making dinner and listening to the day's trial wrap-up. As I wiped the drops of blood off my kitchen counter, immediately I heard the voice of Marcia Clark in my head, cocky and suspicious. "Why so worried about a couple of drops of blood?" she said to me. "What exactly are you trying to hide?"

I was so into the O.J. trial that I found myself praying, as it drew to a close, that another narcissistic celebrity tottering near the edge of a criminal act would volunteer to take the tumble in the name of compelling programming.

After hours of well-intended prepping and cleaning, the folks finally arrived. They seemed unusually glad to see me. They both looked very well, Dad in his tweed jacket with the suede elbow patches, Mom in the kind of velveteen pantsuit that she desperately wished I was wearing. Her short, wavy hair had been newly dyed amber to match her brand-new big, round, tinted Jackie Onassis glasses.

"The seam is coming open under the right arm of your jacket" was the first thing she said when she walked into the room. I didn't even have to raise my arms for her to spot it. She had a gift, a sixth sense, a rare extrasensory flaw-detection ability. I almost gave her a round of applause.

When we all sat down to have our annual glass of champagne, I breathed a big sigh of relief as the flutes passed inspection. I had polished them on and off all day long so compulsively that toward the end I was worried I was just adding smudges and debris or worse, creating scratches.

The toast was a doozy. For a second I thought I had escaped when my father wrested control of it. "To the birthday girl" is all he said. *Whew,* I thought. *Got off easy.* But then *she* started.

She held up her glass and fixed me with a sympathetic gaze that seemed to offer all the pity she had welling up in her soul. Then she said, "Let this be the year that you finally find your true love." Which was bad enough. But she was only warming up.

"Maybe he won't be as handsome as Carl, or as successful, or as talented. Maybe he will be just an average guy who toils at a job he doesn't really like and comes home at night all grumpy, not wanting to talk. Maybe he won't have a lot of interests, or charisma, or fascinating stories to tell. So what if he doesn't have a brilliant intellect and wit, and refuses to read. Perhaps he won't want to do any of the things that you find interesting or exciting. But maybe he will love you. And that will certainly be more than you ever got from Carl."

"Geez, Mom," I said. "Why would anyone want to be loved by that guy you just described?"

Then I realized she had just given me her thumbnail sketch of my father. I glanced over at him to see if he had taken offense at this, but he hadn't noticed. It had just drifted right past him. He thought it was good advice.

"Yes." He nodded. "It's a good idea to learn to settle for less as you get older."

The backsliding really started once Mom handed me the annual gift-wrapped box. I made a big show of removing the wrapping paper in Dad's prescribed manner, pathetically hoping for a little praise. Instead I got a brand-new lecture on how to do the refolding.

"I told you once, I told you a million times, always lead with the existing paper creases," he reminded, even though I was under the impression that I had.

I sat with the naked box on my lap, holding it gingerly as though it contained live snakes, which of course I would have much preferred to the textured wool floral print skirt with a gathered waist and a short jacket with floral braided edging that she insisted I try on right then and there. There was no talking her out of it either. She had been on her good behavior. To refuse would have started a fight.

The outfit was so astonishingly unflattering on me that it almost seemed like a setup to a really, really dark joke, the punch line of which would have arrived when I felt most vulnerable. In a world of my own design, both of my parents would have burst out laughing and then handed me a real present. But no. It was just my mother's annual complete miscalculation of my taste in clothes.

It was almost too painful to look at my reflection in the bathroom mirror. I felt like one of those ballet-dancing hippos dressed in tutus in *Fantasia*.

She had really outdone herself this year. I never looked more overweight or unattractive in my entire adult life. Another year of struggling to build up some self-confidence erased in just a couple of minutes. Twelve months of diet and exercise that seemed never to have happened at all.

All my attempts to raise my self-esteem since my last birthday were colliding in a big twelve-car pileup on the freeway of humiliation. I felt too repulsive to exist in ordinary daylight. The only humane thing to do would be to take up residence in the sewer system, like the Phantom of the Opera.

I briefly searched the ceiling for someplace over which to throw the floral braided edging with which I planned to hang myself. Not finding anything that would support my weight, I took a deep breath and walked back to the living room.

I guess I put a little too much energy into faking a delighted reaction. "You live long enough and things start to change,

Trent. I finally did it," my mother said to my father, winking. "I finally bought her something she actually likes." Her face was lit from inside like a guru after meditation. It was touching. I felt pleased to have given her this imaginary triumph. Right up until she began to insist that I wear it to dinner.

Now I was trapped. There was no path to an excuse. "Wool is a little warm for this time of year" fell on deaf ears. So did "I really would rather save it for a special occasion."

"Nonsense," she said. "It's chilly as hell out. And if this isn't a special occasion I don't know what is."

And from the moment I was forced to leave the privacy of my living room dressed in that outfit, the whole house of birthday cards started to tumble.

First they flatly refused my request to go to a small Italian restaurant in the neighborhood that I knew was always empty.

"We're not going to that lousy dump again," my mother said with finality, insisting on their favorite soulless seafood restaurant chain. It was the kind of place with big laminated menus decorated with clipper ships, the first two pages of which were an exhaustive history of the whaling industry. Dad was once served a piece of sea bass there that he claimed was a full twelve inches. This had some sort of trancelike effect on him, causing him to want to return time after time again, to argue with every succeeding waiter about the fact that the sea bass portions had gotten smaller.

Of course, we ordered another bottle of champagne. But this time Mom made up for her earlier lapse in judgment by proposing the following toast: "Enjoy the rest of your thirties. It's downhill from here."

Lifting the glasses for the toast naturally revealed some

smudges we had forgotten to notice on the restaurant's glass-ware. To say nothing of the spots on the silverware. She re-quested, and received, new glasses and silverware immediately.

And with that, the birthday festivities were up and running. The illusory birthday present triumph had made my parents particularly feisty. So after perusing the menu, they skipped the sea bass argument entirely and jumped feet first into a fight about whether the fresh grilled jumbo shrimp platters were in fact jumbo shrimp or my father's favorite, langostino.

The waiter insisted they were shrimp. My mother insisted they were langostino. My father stood right beside her, pistols blazing. Why this distinction was of such critical importance was beyond my ability to comprehend, but this was just the sort of culinary oversight that drew my parents together. They were frontiersmen, headed for a brave new land of perfect din-ners. When they got there, they would need a scientifically accurate classification of their shellfish preferences, genus, phy-lum, and species. Then armed with this data, they would be able to properly set up their homestead.

"I wonder if they're even fresh," my mother threw in as a bonus taunt.

"Yes, ma'am, all our fish are fresh," said the young waiter.

"Are they fresh?" my mother continued, fixing the poor ju-nior college student with her patented steely stare, one eyebrow raised. "Or are they *fresh frozen*?"

The waiter looked flustered. He started to blush and stam-mer. My parents looked at each other knowingly.

When the orders arrived, everything they both suspected was true. "These are langostino," my father said, "*not* shrimp scampi."

"I'll go back and check with the chef," the now sullen waiter said as he picked up their dishes. Although I'm sure his mood brightened a bit when he got back to the kitchen and it occurred to him that he could drop their entrées on the floor and then sit on them with his bare butt before he brought them back.

"I'm just curious." My father stopped him. "What is your sea bass like tonight? The last few times I ordered it, I was disappointed. But one time, about a year ago . . ."

By now I was quietly time traveling, getting ready to savor the extra seasoning that kitchen staff spit and piss adds to a seafood dinner.

The sea bass story was my cue to take a break. I thought I would go to the ladies' room and hide out there until the eye of the storm blew over.

Of course it was then, dressed in an outfit that made me look like a combination burrito, that I saw Carl and a woman I did not recognize seated at another table. My heart sank. It was the first time I had seen him since the final fuck-yous. He looked trim and fit. He was scrutinizing the menu. Immediately my heart started to pound as my face began to collapse into weepiness.

Naturally the ladies' room was occupied. While at other such times I have been known to duck into the men's room, hoping it's empty, in this case I felt so unattractive that I feared people would think I was the sad recipient of unsuccessful transgender surgery.

This left me trapped in the hall by the ladies' room, knowing that the longer I held up dinner, the more I pissed off my parents. But to escape meant having to deal in some way with Carl.

My options now, as I saw them, were to stop by his table and say hello and have to meet his new girlfriend: out of the question. Or to race past at top speed, as though propelled forward by the importance of my schedule, pretending that I didn't even notice he was there.

But how to deal with his seeing me in the most unattractive clothing I had ever worn in almost four decades on earth? And the fact that his girlfriend, even if she didn't lower herself to making unflattering comments, would definitely be silently gloating as she catalogued my every flaw. Also not an option.

I could stage some kind of a medical alert in the bathroom itself, I thought, by passing out on the sink or on the floor by the toilet. The person who found me would call 911 and para-medics would carry me off on a stretcher with a sheet covering the entire birthday outfit. Clearly this was the smart alterna-tive. That way if Carl saw me he would feel terrible, and living through the rest of tonight's dining combat with the parents would be a moot point. The important thing I had to remem-ber was to leave the door to the rest room wedged open so someone *would* peek inside and find me.

I was mustering up the bravado to go through with this when God smiled on me. Carl got up from his table and dis-appeared. Maybe to use the phone? Maybe to use the men's room? Check his pager? Call his broker? All I knew was time was of the essence.

Skipping my turn at the ladies' room entirely, I put my head down and barreled through the danger zone, back through the stucco archway, to the adjacent room where my parents were still fuming about seafood.

"This is definitely not shrimp scampi," my father said, chewing a forkful and shaking his head. "This is definitely langostino. You'd think a restaurant of this caliber would know what they are serving."

"Sit down and eat your dinner," my mother scolded immediately.

"No one knows anything about anything anymore," said my mother.

My father winked at her and then whispered conspiratorially, "Just between us, langostino is the more expensive of the two. We're actually getting the better end of the deal."

I ate my dinner silently. All I wanted was for us to finish our food and vacate the premises before the happy couple in the next room sensed my presence.

Of course when the check came, we couldn't just get up and leave. No. That was out of the question. My father had to add and re-add the prices of everything multiple times. And naturally he found an error. He always found an error. And an error was an error, even if it was only a matter of seventy-two cents. The waiter was called over. Then the manager. My mother watched, as proud of her man as if he had pulled her from a burning building. Triumphing together over restaurant incompetence was for them the emotional equivalent of the beach makeout scene in *From Here to Eternity.*

The fact that I had been denied access to the ladies' room would have been a greater torment for me physically had I not been so preoccupied by where Carl and his date were in their meal. I kept remembering how Carl was a very rapid eater, almost like a dog. He could inhale a huge steak in two bites. I was in a race against time.

Unless he was on a first date. Then he might order an after-dinner drink, like maybe a glass of port, to try and create the impression that he was not a penny-pinching type A personality who punched holes in walls. If she talked, he might even pretend to be listening.

I had to hope it was a first date. That way I bought myself more time in which to make my escape.

Finally, as was inevitable eventually, my father and the restaurant management agreed that it was okay for us to leave. My mother rose from her chair like a queen on coronation day, savoring a well-earned victory.

Which is when we sashayed right into Carl and his date as they nuzzled near the cash register. The expression on Carl's face could not have been more horrified if he had just encountered a knife-wielding guy in a hockey mask behind his living-room curtains.

"Oh," he said. "Huh! Well . . . !"

"Hi," I said, watching every facial movement either of them made. The whole incident, which probably only lasted about ten seconds, seemed like the longest month and a half of my life.

My mother fixed Carl with an expression indicating that perhaps he was not aware he was pissing on her shoes.

"Oh," she said frostily, and then turned and walked toward the exit. My father followed without saying a word. Not knowing what else to do, I kind of shrugged and held up my hand in a silent gesture of farewell, grateful to be leaving the premises before Carl and company had a chance to examine my outfit more closely.

The girlfriend was never introduced.

"He looked god-awful," my mother said once we got into the car. "He has gotten very pudgy, in my opinion. But did you happen to notice the haircut of the woman he was with? You should think about doing something like that. When your hair gets long, like it is now, it loses its shape."

That I had predicted both of my birthday insults correctly was at least some consolation. I was two for two.

"I told you that Carl liked a more pulled-together look," she said after my silence grew too deafening.

It was still early. The latest, loneliest early evening in my life. And sensing that I desperately wanted to be alone, they decided to come back to my place for a little nightcap.

Following the shrink's advice, I was full into acting laconic. Until we got to my door and there they were: the flowers. The mind-boggling flowers. And the note: Happy Birthday Carl.

Involuntary wooziness and heart palpitations started immediately. This time there were two dozen red roses. Once again they seemed like a message in code. Two dozen red roses. What did that mean in English?

Minutes before, when I had run into him, he hadn't said a thing. His face didn't look like the face of a guy who had just sent flowers. Had I missed that he was actually insulted and was waiting for me to thank him? Was his stunned expression about my lack of gratitude? Did the girlfriend know he had sent them? Was she in on it? Or did he feel guilty because she was there, and therefore couldn't say anything himself without blowing his cover?

Or were they kind of a clandestine but nostalgic thing? Did they mean that he longed for me in spite of her? Maybe she wasn't an official girlfriend at all. Obviously he had sent the flowers before we ran into each other. Or was it possible that he had just sent them a few minutes ago as kind of an apology, post-incident? Should I call him and ask him any or all of these questions?

"He has a lot of nerve," my mother said, shaking her head slowly. "You're well rid of him. I didn't think he looked especially well anyway. He's really getting quite a gut."

I was starting to bask in the warm glow of her insulting remarks about Carl, even loving her for them, when she made one of her famous left turns.

"I've been afraid to ask you all evening because I don't want to get my head bitten off, but your father and I are both wondering if you're seeing anyone new," she said.

"Not really," I said.

They both looked at me with wearisome sadness and sighed.

"A man doesn't like to think that no man wants his daughter," said Dad, making a face that made me think I should offer him sympathy. Perhaps I could help him start a charity fund that would post my picture on plastic containers next to cash registers.

"How about if you accompany me into the bathroom and help me slit my wrists," I said.

"Don't have such a big mouth," he said. "Maybe that's part of the problem. A lot of men don't like a bigmouthed woman."

"Maybe you should join one of those dating services like Doris Olson's daughter Rene, who is forty and has never been married," piped in my mother. "She joined one about a year ago where they send you off with lonely men to some kind of a waffle place. The Waffle Club, I believe they call it. I keep telling Doris it's Jenny Craig she ought to join because the last thing Rene needs is waffles, but what do I know? I'm *always* wrong, as you have taken great pains to remind me many, many, many times over the years."

We were in a metaphorical dark alley and her hand was on her switchblade, but she hadn't yet decided whether or not to push the button that made the blade appear.

In the interest of peace, I decided not to notice she was even armed. I just nodded and made a face that I hoped looked like I was thinking it over.

My mother waited a beat, and then continued. "P.S., she hasn't met anyone yet. But she gets points in my book for trying. I've found that sometimes the illusion of progress is almost as good as progress itself."

When they finally went home, I nearly wept with joy. Then I sat alone, contemplating my fucking flowers. Of course I went right to the Internet to look up the symbolism of red roses. "True love. I love you with all my heart" is what the dictionary said. My eyes began to mist. Was it possible he was really saying this to me?

It was time to acknowledge them. I would be gracious and send Carl a nice note.

The next day I went into a stationery store for the first time in my life and bought a couple of pieces of handmade paper with matching envelopes. They were thicker than pieces of regular paper and had little threads of different pastel colors running through them. I worried as I drove home that maybe I was being *too* nice. I didn't want to appear to be too overwhelmed or trying too hard.

"Dear Carl," I wrote in a handwriting I hoped was casual and yet so filled with character that you couldn't help but think of me as a person with whom you regretted severing relations.

Then I froze. I had no idea what to write. So I switched to notebook paper to make the next few drafts.

"Thank you for the lovely birthday flowers," I wrote.

"Why do you keep sending them?" I added. "I hope you are happy in your new life, whatever it entails. Although I doubt that you are since you are so impossible to please. Are you aware that red roses mean 'I love you with all my heart'? Do you really mean to be saying that to me?"

I balled it up and threw it in the trash.

It's a good thing I was using scratch paper, because at the rate I began throwing rough drafts away, this letter would have cost more in handmade paper than the flowers themselves.

Now I was drawing a blank. I had already said every casual and every profound thing I could think of on this topic.

I could ask him to please stop sending the damn flowers because they were confusing and upsetting. Maybe tell him that if there was something he wanted to say to me, he should just phone me because in its current form the code was indecipherable.

But then a little voice inside my head said, *Hey. Free flowers are free flowers. Keep quiet.*

Suddenly I flashed on a fight we had on one of our early dates: the time when Carl got crabs, then accused me of giving them to him. I took it very seriously, even though I knew I had been with no other men. I sat around trying to think how I could have given him crabs. And I kept on trying to figure it out, even after I realized *I* didn't have any crabs. Maybe, I briefly considered, I had given him *all* my crabs. An entire colony of them had mutinied and leapt, like lemmings, from a low-profile colony somewhere on my body to the hairier, sweatier, and therefore more desirable body of Carl. Just a group of bored crabs, looking for a change of scenery. Who knew the ways of body lice? Maybe, just maybe, this was possible.

That was the genius of Carl and my mother both: They knew how to make others apologize for wrongs they themselves had committed. I remember feeling like I had done something awful. Meanwhile Carl had walked away, not only cleared of all charges, but acting like a victim, sadly wronged.

Where did these people learn how to do this kind of thing? Was it just something you were born knowing? Or was there a class you could sign up for that offered pointers? And was this something I should aspire to?

"Thank you for the lovely birthday flowers" was what I finally wrote. "I still think about you quite a bit. I hope things are going well. If you ever want to get together and talk, you have my number." I signed my name, without a descriptive statement of affection. Love comma was out of the question. Fondly seemed like a ruse. So I took my cue from his annual "Happy Birthday Carl."

I wrote only thank you, followed by my name. As though perhaps I was thanking myself.

What I Learned This Year That I Need to Remember:

1. No more taking the bait from Mom. Even if the fight becomes about not taking the bait.
2. No more dwelling in the past.
3. Try much harder to continue being a vegetarian. This will limit the restaurants the folks can take me to.

4. No more trying to decode the flowers from Carl. If he sends them again, just think of them as a fun, free thing, like a little sample box of cereal or detergent that suddenly appears in the mailbox.

5. Don't make a big deal out of the fact that there were no guys this year. Perhaps that's a better thing than continuing to get involved with guys who exhibit behavior from the beginning that indicates the whole thing is completely hopeless. So try to remember the above as a coping strategy when I am so crazed with horniness that I want to throw myself off a building.

6. No more mumbo jumbo. This means no more calling 900 astrology numbers listed at the end of horoscopes in women's magazines to find out my love forecast. And no more going to psychics, no matter how dicey things get.

First of all, it's just too expensive. But more important, it's too fucking ridiculous for a person with at least an above-average IQ. It makes me feel like there's a life I'm supposed to be having that somehow I'm too incompetent to locate.

I have enough proof by now that it simply doesn't work. Every year I cut out my birthday forecast from the paper. Last year Sydney Omarr said this was going to be a big year for love. October was my special month for marriage.

Apparently some other Aquarius got two big loves and two special marriages. Mine and their own.

That wasn't even the lowest I sank. Oh, no. I brought my own shovel and dug in even lower. I called a telephone psychic. A few times. Well, eight times. And it wasn't just one telephone psychic. It was three different ones.

I realize now I was weak. It was during my warm-sake-in-the-evening phase. Right after Laurel gave me that weird book on how to change the outcome of your life by casting spells and burning candles.

Slowly I noticed that the distance between a glass of warm sake and a telephone psychic was getting shorter and shorter.

At first paying for an optimistic forecast seemed like a reasonable use of my money. Kind of like seeing an overly optimistic shrink who was happy to do all the talking.

The first one was an old lady, specifically selected from the audio menu because of all the people selling this questionable service I thought her voice sounded the most sincere. Of course she claimed to see my soul mate: a guy with a receding hairline who I was going to meet on the concrete steps of a university.

When he never turned up, I called her back in an effort to hold her responsible for this particularly endearing and incredibly inaccurate forecast. This time she saw a George Clooney type that I would run into by the water during the summer months. I was so inspired I made an uncharacteristic number of trips down to the water's edge.

I hope I didn't get skin cancer because he never turned up. What did turn up was the phone bill for $130. There should be a way I can make her repay me for that and all the sunscreen.

The next time I spoke with a woman who called herself Dr. Ruby. I immediately pissed her off when I asked about her doctorate. As a result, she didn't see any love at all in my future. But she did see a new career in air-conditioning repair. I said, "Are you sure? Because I am not a very mechanical person," to which she replied, "Well, that's what my guides are telling me. I get that there's someone who is going to be willing to take you on as an apprentice." That cost me forty dollars, which I should have used to make a down payment on an actual air-conditioning unit since I don't have one.

The third psychic was recommended to me by Ariel, the Spanish teacher, who paid for a reading for me as my birthday present. This woman not only read for her practically every day, but the wife of the head of Polygram Records called this woman and she supposedly picked out a hit single.

Her advice was that I could do whatever I wanted and it would be fine. So I hung up on her. Cost to me: seventy-five dollars. Not even tax deductible.

What I Learned About the Universe and Quantum Physics:

The Hubble telescope brought back evidence this year that proves the existence of black holes in space. They have such powerful gravity that they suck in everything, including light and matter. It is a difficult concept to comprehend although I confess it keeps occurring to me that it may be the human male equivalent of black holes that I have been dating for the past two decades.

Apparently quantum physics is the study of the behavior of the smallest known particles. The Heisenberg uncertainty principle tells us that, unless I am misunderstanding it, everything on the quantum level is uncertain. The behavior of any individual photon is genuinely and inescapably unpredictable.

Yet I predicted with certainty my mother's behavior this year on my birthday. I always thought she was a very dark person. Perhaps this is because she contains relatively few photons. Why does it not surprise me that my mother is the only creature on the planet able to operate outside the laws of quantum physics?

In quantum physics, time is affected by motion. And motion has an equally dramatic effect on space. I am going to pretend that this means that if I just keep moving, my birthday celebrations will become less of a problem.

What I Hope to Learn in the Coming Year:

More on quantum physics. Something about string theory.

... Thirty-nine

It's been a weird year. I guess the big thing was Mom's illness. Although I hardly remember a year when some illness of hers wasn't a centerpiece. And if it wasn't she always made as much as she could out of the threat of a possible recurrence. In our family, illness has always been the most important power chip you can play. If you were sick you had uninterrupted opportunities for leisure, a special, personally designed menu, no obligations at all. Everyone catered to your needs and no one blamed you for anything. It was the path to a life full of polite, well-intentioned, cooperative behavior. We all tried to appear sick as often as possible but no one was remotely as good at it as my mother.

This, however, was her banner year. She really went all out and was hospitalized for quite a long time. When she was first admitted, Dad phoned and asked me to please come right over.

The moment I walked in, Mom looked over at me. "What is she doing here?" she asked Dad as I stood there, stunned.

She took my presence as a sign that her condition had worsened.

But no matter how much doctors tried to make a case that her prognosis was good, she argued that her days were numbered. She seemed to want to dwell in a pit of despair and have us join her there for as long as she cared to stay.

If my father didn't exhibit enough panic or misery on her behalf, she would comment, "Evelyn is waiting in the wings." Then she would shake her head, sigh, and stare mournfully into the middle distance.

Nothing anyone said or did had any effect on her. At lunchtime my father and I went out to a deli and bought her favorite sandwich: a BLT with turkey on rye toast. My father spent a painful amount of time making sure all the specifics were right: Extra-crisp bacon. Romaine lettuce, not iceberg. Turkey sliced extra thin. Grey Poupon mustard. A little mayonnaise, not a lot.

Sitting in her hospital bed, a tray in front of her, I watched her take the sandwich from him, expressionless.

"This turkey is dry" is all she said.

The more her physical condition weakened, the more she became totally obsessed with a competition of some kind she felt she was having with her best friend, Evelyn, for the fair hand of my father. One day when he was out buying her magazines, I tried to talk to her about how silly it all seemed. She just started shaking her head.

"Your father has a thing for her," she told me. "He as much as said he did."

"You're telling me Dad told you he is hot for Evelyn?" I asked. To my surprise, she nodded. It seemed like there was no ceiling and no floor to the self-involved dramas she was willing to stage just to win a totally crazy point. The idea of my father making a sexual move on another woman was impossible to imagine. As close as I could come was to visualize him burying her alive in unnecessary advice.

When the hospital released my mother on her own recognizance, she was on steroids and God knows what else. The effect that the medicine had on her sunny good nature was not positive.

It made me more determined than ever to get off the combat loop with her. After so many years of theatrical illnesses, it was difficult to know how grave this particular crisis was exactly. But I wanted us to have a better relationship for the rest of whatever remaining time she had left.

This was at the root of my motivation for finally hiring a maid. I didn't want my housekeeping to be the source of any more arguments. I thought if I'd put someone else in charge— someone who took cleaning more seriously than I did, someone with whom I could share the blame when my mother reacted to microscopic particles of lint or moisture as though they were dead bodies with chalk outlines, then this would at least eliminate one area of conflict.

In late spring I hired Lolanna, the Central American woman who worked for Laurel. By the time she showed up on a Tuesday morning, I was a nervous wreck. I was so overcome with guilt about foisting what I felt were my housekeeping shortcomings onto another person, especially one from a potentially tragic background, that I almost couldn't leave for work. All those years of listening to my mother disparage the way I cleaned made me embarrassed to let a cleaning professional inspect the premises. Even someone who spoke no English, was in this country illegally, and was grateful to have the job.

So I vacuumed and dusted and washed all the counters the night before she arrived, half expecting her to look at my kitchen, throw her hands up in disgust, and stalk out. It reminded me of when I took a class in college that asked me to give myself a grade. Even though I worked feverishly writing and rewriting an analysis of *Animal Farm* by George Orwell, I also presumed that because it was by me, it deserved a C. When the instructor crossed the C out, wrote in an A, and added the remark "What? Are you kidding?" I worried that he was being sarcastic.

I don't know if Lolanna had an obsessive-compulsive problem or was a delusional overachiever as I was, or if I really did dwell in the belly of the beast like my mother said, but her cleaning was so unbelievably thorough that by the time she left that first day there were no more numbers on my oven dials.

By the third week there was not a number on a dial anywhere in my house. Stove and microwave all denuded. Every appliance I owned was number- and word-free. No more words indicating the cycles on my washing machine. No more numbers indicating stations on my radio.

"Buy some new stuff. It's all digital" is what Laurel had to say about it. Instead I tried to figure out how much of an unmarked turn would get me to Rinse or Bake or KPWR-106.

That's when my things started disappearing. It turned out she wasn't stealing them. She was breaking them, and then hiding the pieces. By the end of the month I had no vases or wineglasses. I would find the broken items stashed in the back of a cupboard or drawer, sometimes with a place mat or a napkin draped over them to keep their little corpses warm.

I really wanted to fire Lolanna and go back to my filthy old ways. I thought of pleading poverty and offering a giant severance check. But the several times I tried, she looked at me like a human cocker spaniel. So guileless and well intended was the expression in her big brown eyes that if she had brought me a tennis ball in her mouth, I would still be standing there throwing it for her.

I briefly considered moving and not leaving a forwarding address. But in the end I opted for buying plastic glasses and vases. I guess I liked the feeling that I might make out okay in the cleanliness department if my mother dropped by unannounced. And that went a long way toward balancing out the anguish of discovering that Lolanna had put my cashmere sweater in the dryer, and now it was the size and shape of a pot holder. The next time someone threw a surprise party for Malibu Barbie, I had the perfect present.

Yet so determined was I to solve my problems with my mother, I even hired someone to replaster the holes Carl had punched in the walls. I also began to carry a notebook in which I could jot down possible argument topics, as they occurred to me, so I could consult with the shrink about battle strategies.

The trouble turned out to be that when the scenarios played out in real life, Mom would throw left hooks. When she was in her element, and picking surprise fights was definitely her element, she could be very creative.

For instance, when she came to visit last summer, I had just resumed painting seriously again. I shouldn't have mentioned it at all, but we were dangerously out of neutral topics. It was the only decoy I had to avert yet another depressing examination of my love life.

Of course, once I brought it up, she and my father both wanted to see my paintings. This made my blood run cold. The last time I had shown them a painting I had completed, my mother looked at me, shrugged her shoulders, and said, "Well, I don't happen to care for it. But I pray I'm wrong."

I wasn't prepared to have my new work disemboweled.

So I replied with something it seemed to me that the shrink might have advised me to say.

"I will show you my new paintings," I said, "but since I'm very thin-skinned, will you do me a favor and be really tactful? Pretend you like them even if you hate them? That is all I ask."

My mother looked at me, her face stiffening into a dead-eyed tragedy mask.

"What are you saying?" she said, deeply disappointed. "That's what has become of our communication? It's limited now to superficial bullshit and lies? You're telling me that you want me to be dishonest with my own daughter? It just so happens that art is a field I know something about. If I can't criticize you, what are we supposed to talk about? The weather?"

"Well, we can talk about the weather if you like," I said. "Or maybe there's some additional topic we could find if we gave it more thought. How about current events? Or books we have read?"

She began to shake her head, then rose and went into the adjoining room. There she sat, alone, staring up at the ceiling, on the verge of tears.

"I thought we agreed that you were going to knock this shit off" is what my father said to me as he exited the room to go comfort her. "I don't know what kind of thrill you get making your sick mother cry. You're not earning your living as a professional artist. Why do you have to make such a big deal about what she says about your paintings? What do you care?"

I was the bad guy. I had hurt her feelings by trying to keep her from hurting my feelings. My parents were an unbeatable two-man tag team for low self-esteem.

I think it was around this time that I started seeing Trevor. That I was numb emotionally certainly was a factor. It had been a year and a half since I had sex. There was nothing at all like love on the horizon.

And I was also getting really sick of listening to all the single women I know talk about looking for good guys and not finding them. It was like listening to vegetarians talk about ways to cook tofu. "Marinate it in teriyaki sauce." "Grill it with a garlic sauce!" "Sauté it in black bean sauce and green onions with a dash of sherry!" But in the end, it was still the same old tofu.

I was also beginning to suspect that a lot of my single friends were kind of strange in their own right. I wouldn't have wanted to date any of them either.

And then my friend Laurel started playing the Internet. Before she even told me about him, she snuck off and married a guy she met in a chat room. She had only known him two weeks.

"Two weeks?" I said to her. "You're not serious. You've only known him two weeks!"

"But I e-mailed him for at least a month before that," she said.

This really upset me. On the one hand, it said to me that possibly there were opportunities all around me that I was ignoring. That meant there were uncomfortable new things I had to learn how to do. On the other hand, it said to me that everything I thought was sane or crazy in dating might be completely irrelevant now. How could a seemingly smart woman make a choice like that in two weeks?

I'd gotten even worse at evaluating love between other people. This year especially, every time I opened the *National Enquirer* and read a story about how two actors who met on a movie had found a love that rocked the ages, I bought the whole story lock, stock, and barrel. I would immediately envy them, imagining that they knew important things about love and life and spontaneous emotion that I would never know. I marveled at the telephoto shots of their passionate kisses on tropical islands, even when the captions made fun of their too heavy midsections. I gazed doe-eyed at the personalized tattoos they got proclaiming their new love for each other. And I would continue to believe in this drama until the time I read that mutual restraining orders had been filed.

And it wasn't only with movie stars that I had a tendency to make irrational leaps of faith where other people's love affairs were concerned. This year it seemed like as soon as I accepted a couple anywhere as being a good love model, it was only a short while until I started hearing rumors that things were not what they seemed. And the next thing I knew, one or both of them would call me to tell me that the other one was an asshole. Then it was up to me to decide which of these Designated Assholes was still my friend.

Still I was very freaked-out when Laurel snuck off to Vegas without telling a single soul and married Internet Boy. And even more freaked-out when I phoned her to talk about it and he picked up the phone.

"Who is this?" he asked.

"A friend of hers. And who are you?" I countered.

"I'm her new husband," he said.

"Wow" is all I could say. "Well, congratulations. I think."

I guess that wasn't the most ringing endorsement or biggest show of support I could have offered.

"You can be happy for us," he said. I didn't like the feeling of being pushed into a positive emotion by a total stranger. Which is when he hung up on me.

Thinking we had been disconnected, I called right back.

"How dare you talk to me like that in my own home!" he screamed at me. "I live here now. This is my home, too. And I don't like your tone," he added.

This time *I* hung up on *him*.

What in the world was Laurel thinking—marrying a guy who ushered in their life of bliss by hanging up on her friend?

But the more I thought about it, the more I began to think that even though her relationship seemed completely screwed up, and almost certainly doomed . . . maybe it was good. At least she had new activity in her life. Maybe my mother was right. Maybe the illusion of progress was as good as progress itself.

Maybe I needed to take more risks. Maybe a checkered, goofy love life full of tragedy and strife, full of hideous lows and delusional highs, was better than a long blank period jampacked with nothing. Maybe this was the message the universe was trying to give me. It was instructing me to stop worrying about trying to get things right and just do something, anything. Be vulnerable. Don't think so much. Live.

With this new attitude in place, my policy was going to be to say yes to things that deserved a no. So I agreed to go to dinner with this guy Daniel, who I had met at a dinner party with the And-Michaels about a year before. (At that point the And-Michaels were Lynnie and Michael, who I've known since college, Susan and Michael from the English department, and Dawn and Michael from across the street. James and Michael weren't together yet and only James was there.) I didn't sense any particular chemistry with Daniel. I never feel very chemically charged around guys who get manicures. But I was trying out my new devil-may-care thing. What the hell! Live and let live! Although that all changed in an instant when he phoned to make the arrangements, and he didn't get my name right. My heart, which hadn't been exactly what you would call buoyant before, went ahead and sank.

Other bad signs quickly followed. The second thing he said, after we sat down to dinner, right after we placed our orders, was that he had to be home by nine so he wouldn't miss *Seinfeld.* Anyone, in any situation, who is running home from a real-live personal encounter to *anything* on TV . . . well, I not only stopped listening to him after that, it was as though his head had morphed into a big steaming bucket of fresh cow manure. I focused instead on the conversation at the next table about the possible remarriage to a much younger woman of the friend of a woman with bright blue bangs. I ceased making any eye contact with Daniel, but I'm not sure he even noticed. He went on and on about his fantastic new cell phone and all the incredible things it could do and what an amazing deal he had gotten. During this portion of the dinner, I came up with an idea for a great new art assignment: Draw an outline of two heads and, inside comic-strip-type word balloons, make a collage or drawing that shows in images what sort of conversation the people think they are having, then write below what they are really saying.

The bad news was that I tuned him out so effectively, I gave him the impression we got along really well. He kept calling and calling for a couple of weeks after that.

I avoided his first few calls by screening them on the answering machine. When I finally picked up, I did the thing where I told him I had gotten back with an old boyfriend. This caused him to lecture me at length about how I was making the biggest mistake of my life, which was kind of uplifting. I thought to myself, *Well, good. If this is the biggest mistake I ever make in my life, I am in really great shape.*

That very same weekend I met Trevor at Amanda's party. I think maybe the Daniel fiasco is why I gave myself permission to flirt with another completely hopeless case. I was proving just how much Daniel had underestimated the kind of impressive mistakes I still had ahead of me.

Having previously put in a full year on the "learn to know when something is hopeless and then don't start anything hopeless" program, the minute I looked into Trevor's eyes I saw a neon sign flashing, "Hopeless! Totally hopeless!" Which is of course precisely the same moment that the dumb girl started to lecture.

"Oh well, what the fuck" is how she began.

"You haven't had any sex at all in over a year, for God's sake. Are you never going to ever have any sex again, ever? Doesn't your reproductive system atrophy or something if you go too long in a state of total deprivation? I'm sure I read somewhere that if you go too long without sex it's structurally bad for your circulation."

Well, I started thinking to myself, *what if I go into this with both eyes wide open? Couldn't I try to handle this situation like a guy would? Couldn't that work? If I had no illusions at all? If I re-*

minded myself constantly that I should expect nothing, then it wouldn't have to be defined as hopeless, would it? Then it could be just defined as fun.

Trevor was a kind of strange, froggy-looking, bug-eyed guy but he had a lot of magnetic pull in a growly, disapproving sort of way. Growly and disapproving was of course narcotic to me. He was one of those guys whose confidence in himself made him look sexier and sexier as you got to know him.

From the beginning it was hard to harbor any illusions because he was a member of one of nature's most dangerous species, second only to the hooded cobra. He was a poet and a musician. He had a small, loyal following. Alternative magazines that liked ornery purists liked him.

He'd just put out a CD of his work for which Amanda's husband's law firm had done the contracts: part spoken word, part songs. Twice the danger, twice the trouble at bargain-basement prices. Just back from a few months on the road, opening for bigger bands, he was feeling really restless and unsettled. He had an appealing melancholy vibe, like he was looking for someone who would understand.

"He asked me if I knew anyone I could introduce him to," Amanda whispered to me, as though she thought he might be a good catch. But then again, Amanda is a woman who married a guy who makes frequent appearances in a rectangular box on CNBC as one of those rabid, rage-filled lawyers who argue with Alan Dershowitz. She thought *he* was a good catch, too.

We got off to a bad start. I kind of pissed Trevor off when I told him I'd like to hear his work. Apparently I was already supposed to have it memorized.

Disappointed, he said he'd send me a CD if I gave him my

address. So I wrote it on the back of a supermarket receipt I found in my purse. And as almost an afterthought I also added my phone number. Just for the hell of it. Part of the new, riskier, friskier me.

When I left the party, he volunteered to walk me out to my car. Then while we were standing there, rapidly running out of things to talk about, he suddenly kissed me. It kind of came out of the blue. And it had an oddly practiced feel to it, a degree of sexual competence that stood out among generic kisses.

Which is not to say that everyone else had been totally inept. But this was the first time it ever occurred to me while I was kissing someone that he seemed to have had a ton of practice. The way he moved one of my arms behind my back. The way he was in control, like he knew what came next.

I thought, *Just relax and enjoy it. Think of it as a counterpoint to all these years of fumbling. A free dinner at Spago after a decade of McDonald's Happy Meals.*

The effect it had on my libido was so dramatic that I didn't know how to act. The dumb girl wanted to drag him into the backseat of my car, pin him down so he couldn't escape, and start to unbutton his clothes. But my smarter self told me to get into my car *alone* immediately and get myself home.

I could hardly see straight trying to drive. A hornet's nest of hormones were suddenly unleashed and were trying to take over my being like the angry zombies did in *Night of the Living Dead.* They were pounding at the doors, staring in the windows, making horrible moaning noises.

My mind was in such a libido-driven stupor that I thought I might have a message waiting on my machine from him when I got home, if I didn't plunge my car off a cliff or into a tree first. The memory of the heat that came off that kiss was like the heat off a spa with a broken thermostat. If I felt it that strongly, I figured he probably did, too.

But no. He never called.

I quickly reminded myself that none of this mattered. I was lucky. All I had done was accidentally avert a bunch of trouble. Even though it did occur to me that it was a danger sign of gigantic proportions that I was already having this kind of discussion with myself before I'd ever slept with him.

It was also very suspect how I pretended that going in and out of eight different rare-CD stores trying to buy his work was the kind of casual, easygoing, everyday activity that I always undertook. Suddenly I was some kind of musicologist.

I think I might have liked his work anyway, despite the fact that he had a sort of strangled, reedy, high-pitched, nasal voice that reminded me a teensy bit of a singing Elmer Fudd. He played guitar, saxophone, and keyboard and he wrote a lot of his songs with a group of people whose names I didn't recognize. But I couldn't help but notice that the songs he wrote alone were whiny, one-sided laments about how dark, depressed, and unhappy he was. To hear him tell it, no matter how hard he tried, cold, cruel women kept kicking him in his poor, battered heart, then stomping it into the ground for no reason at all. Wicked witchy women in primary-colored dresses makin' promises they wouldn't keep. Could not, would not, give him what he wanted and needed. Kept on leaving him out in the cold. Kept on turning him out in the rain. Saw him blowing like a leaf in a hailstorm and just kept walkin'. Kept on yearning, ever yearning, to be free, free, free.

So where did he get all that practice with sex? is what I found myself thinking. *Where did all that confidence come from if all he ever meets are these power-crazy, rejecting, witchy women?*

The truth was that I couldn't tell objectively if I even liked his new CD because the audio contact with the emotion in his voice when he sang had a Pavlov's dog effect on me, causing me to connect somehow physically with the brain cells that remembered that hot kiss. I think I would have liked it equally well if he had been singing in a Hungarian falsetto with a mouth full of rye crisp.

The more I listened to it, the more turned-on I was getting.

Now I finally understood why getting involved with a musician was so dangerous. With a guy who has a regular job, like, say, a teacher or a salesman, you have to use your imagination to provide yourself with the necessary obsessional data. You have to try to remember what they said or did or how they looked. You need photographs. Or letters. You need to drive your friends crazy seeking out their opinions on your anecdotes, making them listen to you tell them over and over. You have to use applied teenage logic to make the songs on the radio seem to be about you.

But this guy came complete with his own personal sound track full of tormented laments for every occasion. I could take him into the bath or along in the car. It took pointless, one-sided obsession to a whole new level.

The more I listened, the more turned-on I was getting. Even though it occurred to me on more than one occasion that I was listening to the sad tales of a self-absorbed adolescent. When our affair finally went to hell in a hand basket . . . and there was no chance that it wouldn't . . . I would never even be able to get any sympathy from my friends. How can you get them to empathize with a decision to get involved with a guy who titled his first album *Song of the So-Called Asshole*?

Nevertheless, the dumb girl who I had hoped was dead was

definitely back and in glowing good health. Apparently she was
willing to work golden time for regular pay as she tried to talk
me into writing him a note to say I liked the CD as a way to try
and provoke some interaction.

She was correct that I really wanted him to call me. But I
didn't want to seem like some stupid fan begging for attention.

I wasn't as clearheaded about my intentions when the dumb
girl talked me into going to a club where he was playing, pretending I always went out at night alone to clubs. She thought
it might be okay to maybe go backstage after the show and say
hello. And I almost went through with it, too. Until, when I
was buying a ticket, I noticed at least three different versions of
myself standing in line, dressed up and looking like kiss survivors.

It was so humiliating I made a big show of checking my
watch impatiently to indicate to no one in particular that the
person I was supposedly meeting was late. *I had better go look
for him,* I tried to make my face say. And then I turned on my
heel, ran out of the club, and sped home like I was driving the
pace car in the Indianapolis 500.

About three weeks later I still hadn't heard from him. I was
doing my best to pretend I had forgotten about him altogether.
On this particular evening I was on the couch making yet
another attempt to understand quantum physics. And toward
this end I was trapped on a page of another book that was supposed to be a clear, easy explanation for beginners, even though
it contained sentences like "In a quantum mechanical experiment, the observed system, traveling undisturbed between the
region of preparation and the region of measurement, develops
according to the Schrödinger wave equation." I was reading

this sentence over and over, pretending not to be fixated on Trevor's CD in the background, when the phone rang.

"I finally found that scrap of paper with your address on it," Trevor said to my answering machine. "I would have called before. . . . Sorry it's taken me so long. . . . I thought I would finally get around to sending you my new CD."

"Hi," I said, picking up the phone before he hung up. "I already bought your new CD. I've really been enjoying it."

"Really!" he said, sounding pleased. I imagined him doing the thumbs-up as he comprehended that I was easy pickings. "What are you doing right now?" he asked me.

"Oh, just reading up on quantum physics," I said, wondering if that made me sound like a woman of deep and profound wisdom and mystery, or a geek.

"Have any interest in going out to get something to eat?" he replied, as if I'd never said anything.

Then something in his voice reminded me of that kiss and the next thing I knew the dumb girl and her zombie hormones had taken over the controls. I had forgotten I ever purchased another book on quantum physics.

From the minute I met him for dinner, it was a given I was going to have sex with him. It was going to be great sex and I was going to get hurt. How badly was up to me.

I am sorry to say I was way too happy to see him. He looked really good in his denim jacket and white T-shirt. He was much tanner than I remembered. The growth of beard he was sporting made him look ruggedly handsome.

"Have you been out hiking or something?" I naïvely asked.

"Self-tan." He whispered, "The spray kind. By Clarins."

I was already so enamored that I didn't even register what a lame thing this was to say. Instead, I liked him for his honesty and his ability to show his dumb, vain side. I was ready to embrace his every eccentricity.

Almost immediately I began lecturing myself about remaining aloof in the face of a losing battle.

Remember that you have already agreed to be like the man in this scenario, I reminded myself. *If you start acting like a woman and doing that bonding bullshit, you are cream cheese on toast. You are dead meat. Game over.*

We sat and ate Mexican food. He told me about going on tour. He said he liked changing locations constantly, meeting new people in every city. Meeting new women in every city.

I don't think in the whole two hours he asked me a single question about myself.

But when he pushed his knee up next to my knee under the table, the dumb girl stopped listening to my nervous asides entirely. The electricity coming off that knee began keeping me from hearing a single thing that was coming out of his mouth. It was like a downed power line had disrupted his transmission. Now I was watching TV with the sound turned off.

My knee, on the other hand, was on fire. Definite third-degree burns. I had a certifiable case of volcano knee. Flaming knee jubilee.

"If you want to do this, you can do this," I reminded the dumb girl. "Understand that you have my permission. But you can*not* be dragging *my* feelings into your dopey maneuvers. You have to maintain perspective. Stay aloof."

"I can do this," the dumb girl said with impressive confidence. "Plenty of people do this all the time and so can I." I hoped she meant we.

We went over to his apartment. It didn't even bother me that he lived in a miserable dump that had never known the hum of a vacuum cleaner. Or that he also had the mandatory single-guy assortment of dead plants sitting in parched potting soil.

I was on top of it all. I would buy him a really big plant to remember me by—like a ficus or a rubber plant in a thirty-inch pot. I would leave behind the biggest dead plant his apartment had ever known when I finally made my exit.

Of course, the sex was awesome as advertised. It was like being part of a really good chemistry experiment. Everything was a turn-on. It felt like the sexual equivalent of a big, cool, chocolate shake. Delicious, with minimal nutritional value, consequences to come later.

Afterward, he sang me a new song he had written. It was almost a beautiful moment, until I realized the lyrics he was singing were about a cruel woman who was hunting him, toying with him, trying to destroy him.

"How is it that a sexy guy like you has met so many cruel women?" I asked him.

"I've been having trouble with women my whole life," he said, wounded and yet hopeful. Like he wondered if I was going to hurt him, too. His remark was perfectly calculated to make the dumb girl inside of me try to give him the impression that now he was safe with me. *I wouldn't hurt you,* I felt my face trying to convey. Even though I knew perfectly well that I, and not he, was the one who was in danger.

In a way, watching an attractive, potentially dangerous guy play guitar is a little like watching a tiger agree to do tricks for his trainer. You know that they could just turn and kill you. But you're so flattered and pleased that instead they agreed to stand on a decorative box and wave and count for the crowd that for a while you forget how big the scary part of them really is.

He was really wired that first night. After exhausting sex so hot I was afraid some of my body parts might have melted, he jumped up, got dressed, and went out to an all-night market. He bought us tons of food. Steaks. Many bags of spaghetti. I thought he must have the biggest appetite. But he never cooked any of it.

We were so completely on fire that I refused to let anything dubious or strange he did get me down. Like when he took me over to the computer to show me his Internet chat room. Okay, yes, that seemed a little bit egomaniacal. Especially when he mentioned he'd had sex with most of the women online. "Read between the lines of their comments and you can tell which ones I fucked," he said. Like I wanted to sit there and analyze the postings of a bunch of ridiculous fan-club members.

I decided to pretend he was kidding around. I couldn't face the idea that he wasn't.

Some small amount of what was left of my instinct for self-preservation told me it would be better if I didn't sleep over. Snuggling in bed offered too many additional opportunities for bonding. I didn't want the chance to watch him asleep, looking vulnerable, angelic, magnetic. I didn't want to somehow find myself thinking I loved him.

Plus I knew I'd never get any sleep. I'd be waking up all night long to sneak off to the bathroom and fix my makeup.

Nevertheless, the reality is that when you like a thing you like it. Whether you want to pretend you can control how you feel about liking it or not. And from the first time I had sex with Trevor, and hung out with him, I liked it. I didn't want to have to put limits on how much. This, of course, came to define my problem.

We started to have sex a second time in the elevator of his building on the way down to the parking garage. It finished up, a little too fittingly, in back of a Dumpster on the hood of my car at three in the morning. When I got home later, I realized I had the most romantic souvenir of all: hood grime on my butt.

Afterward, we kissed good-bye and he waved and reboarded the elevator by himself, perfectly happy to send me off into the city in the middle of night, all alone.

"Talk to you soon" is what he always said when we parted company. This turned out to mean whatever he needed it to: Later that same day. Or in a month. Or in a week and a half.

But so what? I would say to myself. *I always knew what I was getting into. At least I am living my life on the edge. At least I am taking risks. Isn't this a better way to live than doing nothing?*

On the drive home I turned the radio up really loud in the hope that it would invade my body enough to change my DNA. Maybe there was some chance that it would help me convince myself I really didn't give a flying fuck.

This detachment lasted about thirty-six hours. After that a wave of obsession came in like a tsunami to replace it. And with the obsession came a lot of counterproductive reasoning. The dumb girl's imagination was very sophisticated when it came to obsessing. It was the thing she did best.

"Maybe after a while, if you hang in there, he will get hooked on you the same way you are hooked on him," she offered, as though she was from some alternate universe where this was a possibility. "After all, he is only human. You guys are really hot together. And you can't be that hot with someone without feelings creeping in. It's not possible. Ask anyone."

She and Laurel both believed this to be the truth, and they both lectured me about it regularly. "Plus," they would both add, "if you need to connect to him sooner, what is stopping *you* from calling *him*?"

Which I finally did. After a long talk with them both about how it was okay because we weren't in a traditional relationship, so there weren't really any rules, therefore there weren't any that could be broken. That made sense to me and the dumb girl at the time.

He was always incredibly nice about calling right back. And he always had a semiplausible excuse that I was willing to buy. Might as well. What choice did I really have? I knew I didn't have any power.

One time when I hadn't heard from him for about a week, he said he had just gotten back to town. He'd been off performing somewhere and visiting some friends. Of course, he had never mentioned beforehand that he was planning to leave. And after he returned, he never said whether the friends he was visiting were male or female or a delightful combination of both. Hey, he was under no obligation to clear his every move with me. Why make a big thing out of it, right?

Naturally, he couldn't make plans to get together. But he would as soon as things settled down. What needed to settle down I didn't know.

He would talk to me soon.

This time "soon" turned out to be six days later when he called me from his car phone at seven-thirty on a Thursday. He was about a block from my house. He wanted to know if I was available in about an hour, after he finished getting a facial.

I was tempted to say no, just to make it seem like I had an agenda of my own. I mean, a guy getting a damn facial is kind of a turn-off. I could have said I already had plans. But of course I was thrilled that he called. I was starving for human contact *and* sexual contact.

The dumb girl had her hand over my mouth and wouldn't let me back off. So I pretended that I was a person like he was: Spontaneous. Loose. Looking for a good time. Obsessed with skin exfoliating. Hanging around after work ready to take the best offer that presented itself.

I told him he could come over. But then, so as not to seem like a complete and total chump, I went to the market on the corner and bought myself some having-a-full-life-without-you decoys: a dozen roses and a pack of Camels—souvenirs from some mythological suitor who just happened to leave them sitting out on a table the last time he was visiting. Certainly I would have cleaned them off if I'd have known that Trevor was coming to visit. But he really hadn't left me with that option since he dropped by on such short notice. Who knew what you might find at my house if you just dropped by? You took your chances. I lived fast.

Of course, Trevor never noticed. My details were not of any particular interest to him. I doubt it ever occurred to him to care. I ended up giving the Camels to a homeless guy. I should have sent the roses to Carl.

Even more tragically, I was so glad to see him when he appeared at my doorstep that we almost had sex before he got through the front door. To slow things down and make the evening last a little longer, I browbeat him into seeing a movie first. That way he would at least have to spend some time with me.

We decided to see the last of the *Halloween*s (*The Curse of Michael Myers*), which quickly rose to the top of my list of the most erotic films of all time. I'd never made out to a decapitation before. But since virtually all contact with Trevor made me hot, I hardly noticed that most of the cast who were alive in the beginning of the film were now leaking corpses.

We left before the movie was over, then started having sex in his car, right in the parking lot. I kept getting sun visor injuries, so we detoured into the horrible no-tell motel directly next door to the theater instead.

It was a grotesque place. The Bluebird Inn . . . a place so un-bluebirdlike it made bluebirds seem scary. If Michael Myers and his curse had been checking into the next room, it wouldn't have surprised me.

There was a mirror over the bed, which turned out to be the opposite of an erotic aid because it was damaged in some kind of strategic way that had warped it into a fun-house mirror, thereby making my legs appear to be joined to my hips at right angles. But even seeing a reflection of myself staring down from the ceiling with accordion pleats in my thighs didn't dampen my ardor.

Or the fact that we dared not fall asleep on that potentially infected bed for fear of being carried off by a giant herd of bacteria. Or the fact that I couldn't have an orgasm because I was too preoccupied with trying to stay detached. Although I must say I have rarely been in better faking form.

By the time he dropped me off at my house, I realized I had gotten no clues from him about anything. No new information. No plans for the future. No plans at all.

"I'll talk to you soon," he said as he kissed me good-bye at the car.

"Soon like later this week?" I said, knowing I was stepping into dangerous territory. "If it's not too pushy, how are we defining 'soon'? Does it mean next month? Next Christmas? Any ideas at all?"

"Soon," he said, grinning, and then giving me another kiss on the mouth.

"Doesn't a really hot kiss mean he has to be feeling *something*?" I asked Laurel. "You can't have a kiss that hot if he feels nothing, can you?"

"I think it probably does mean that he has feelings for you," she said. "That's how I knew it was the right thing to do to marry Internet Boy."

More words of wisdom. A month later she moved out of his house. Two months later she filed for an annulment.

Meanwhile I settled down to wait for "soon." And this time "soon" meant a week from Thursday.

It was a very long eight days, filled with lectures to myself about how as long as I wasn't involved everything would be okay. Counteracted by eight days full of listening to his CD while I pretended that it didn't mean anything to me because I was mainly preoccupied with my own life.

By now I was scrupulously examining the lyrics of his songs for clues about who he was and what he did with himself all day long. I became obsessed with the idea of setting up a hidden camera that would allow me to watch him move through his day in fast-forward. Would I see him going from woman to woman? Did they show up at his house and spend a forty-five-minute hour like they might if they had a shrink appointment? Would the film reveal the different ones as they crossed paths in the parking garage, never knowing or even suspecting they were looking at the next appointment as she arrived? Or was the missing piece that he had so much anxiety and depression that he couldn't communicate? Was it remotely possible he was so busy writing music that he spent his days alone?

Oh, I had plenty of questions. When he whined that his aching heart was like a battlefield, why had he neglected to mention who it was who first declared war? Exactly what really happened to all those girls he claimed tortured him because they just wanted to be free? Did they really demand their freedom? Or was it forced on them when they couldn't get a hold of him? Maybe they all just went nuts trying to figure out how long he meant by "soon."

Finally, finally, the light went on. The girls in all of his songs were really him.

The dumb girl said something smart. Like the monkeys with the typewriters who would eventually write Shakespeare, it had to happen sooner or later. She pointed out to me that I only saw him on weekday evenings.

"Is he secretly married?" I wondered. "Is he living with someone? Does she only get weekends off? Does he have whole solar systems of girlfriends or is he a sun with an assortment of faithful rotating planets? Or is it that he had a main girlfriend and a lot of clandestine other ones, more like asteroids and comets, most just his dirty secrets?

Which category was I? Or was I too insignificant to even have a category? Maybe I was just dark matter, or a brown dwarf. That was certainly what I felt like.

And why did I care? I wasn't even supposed to care. I had promised myself I wouldn't care.

On the eighth day of "soon," he agreed to meet me at the art museum. My premise was that I was trying to force our relationship to expand a little, although I didn't exactly go about it in the most prudent possible way. The dumb girl talked me into showing up in a dress with no underwear.

Naturally our chemistry ignited instantly. He pulled me behind a Rodin sculpture and slid his hand up my dress. Next thing I knew we were having sex in a ladies' room stall.

After that, as we walked around and I pretended to look at the paintings, all I could really hear was the dumb girl pitching a total fit. She was feeling bruised and romantic, exactly the way she was forbidden to feel. And on the worst possible timetable, too. The museum was getting ready to close.

"How many other women do you have in your life?" she asked him, as he pressed himself against me on the way down in the elevator. He grinned and looked away.

"A few" is what he said.

"How many is a few?" I heard her ask him. "Or is that one of your words that is open to interpretation, like the word 'soon'?"

"Do you really have to know the answer to that question?" he countered.

I began to think that maybe I didn't need the answer. Which of course is when I got it anyway.

"Actually, I am kind of engaged to be married," he told me, "but that doesn't have to affect our relationship. The woman I'm engaged to is very cool with me doing whatever."

To say this put a damper on things is to understate. I felt like I suddenly had my very own weather system. There was a small and totally portable thunderstorm attached to the back of my neck and hovering over my hair. Everything in my brain that wasn't tied down to a synapse was whipping around in cyclonic winds.

As we began to walk to the car, I could hear the dumb girl

thinking about giving it one last try. Poor thing, she was actually trying to look for a silver lining.

"Is that who you see on Saturdays?" she asked.

"Well, yes," he said. "But there are others. You know about the road, right?" he said, as though I was Willie Nelson.

"You mean, girls on the road?" I said, sounding like someone who was too dumb to even hang out with the dumb girl in my head. I was an anachronism from a previous century.

"Well, yes," he said, "there are the ones that come to the shows. The ones I just see for one night. And then there are the ones I call whenever I get into their town. Some of them I've been seeing a couple times a year for the past ten years. Those are the ones you were reading in my chat room."

I stared at him, mute, to let him know I had neither the time nor the inclination to be reading postings in his stupid fucking chat room. Even though, of course, I actually had sifted through them pretty thoroughly.

After that I stopped seeing him. I don't know who initiated the stoppage. But once it ground to a halt, no one bothered to put the key back in the engine and turn it again. For a brief moment I thought that maybe *soon* wasn't up yet. But this time "soon" meant never again.

It was right about this same time that Mom got out of the hospital again and under doctor's orders was forced to join a "wellness group." She did so only reluctantly because she didn't approve of therapy. "How can they claim to help me when they don't even *know* me?" she said with much disdain. "Why would I fit their formulas? Am I not a unique individual?" That was Mom, willing to flick off the entire history of psychology and literature like an annoying mosquito.

I don't really know what went on in the wellness group itself, except that they gave her a stuffed monkey that was supposed to represent her inner child. It was an ocher-colored plush toy with a huge head and a big, weird grin they asked her to call Little Lily.

During this period when I went home to visit, I found her unusually chatty. The influence of (or maybe the attention from) the wellness group had made her more self-examining, not so judgmental. She seemed for a moment to blossom in a positive way.

I was pleasantly surprised to find myself having a conversation with her that seemed both casual and intimate. It reminded me of the kinds of conversations I generally had with actual friends, where you speak about feelings and thoughts and no one scrutinizes you like you are an incomplete science project.

True, there was a downside to some of this newfound self-examination. Like her cheery revelation that in fact she never really wanted to have kids. Not what I'd call a really heartwarming topic, yet in a weird way, it didn't upset me that much to hear her say it. At least now she was offering a window into why she acted the way she did. At least now I could kind of comprehend her.

Wow, I thought, *this is an amazing change, and a poignant one.* The idea that I would begin to know my mother up close and personal after a lifetime of distance and criticism was almost more than I could bear.

But it seemed correct and way overdue. After all, I reasoned, that's what happens in every movie. People who could never communicate have a meaningful emotional breakthrough in the eleventh inning of life.

Just thinking about it made my eyes fill with tears. I wanted to say something reinforcing. I wanted to hear her thoughts, even if they were upsetting.

So I turned to her and said, "Mom, I want to tell you how much I enjoyed our conversation just now. When you talk to me like this, it makes me feel very close to you."

"*Just now?*" she said. "This is the only time you feel close to me? *Just now?* Well, because I talked to you like this *just now* doesn't mean I always have to talk to you like this."

And true to her word, she never talked intimately to me that way again.

A few weeks later she went into the hospital and never came out. I only saw her one other time, when I showed up for an unscheduled visit.

She hardly looked at me when I came into the room. Then she picked up Little Lily, the weird, grinning, stuffed monkey with the big head that represented her inner child, and threw it across the room. "Fuck Little Lily," she said. "Fuck Little Lily."

After I got the call that things had taken a turn for the bleak, I rushed to meet Dad at the hospital. Racing toward her room, I encountered him walking back toward me from the other direction.

"She's gone," he said to me. "Kidney failure. Do you want to go in and say good-bye?"

I didn't. The idea of spending time with my mother in a state that offered even fewer possibilities for communication made no sense at all.

Dad and I drove around town in silence for the rest of the day, making funeral arrangements.

The only part that made me feel weird was when he ordered the flowers: two bouquets of red roses, exactly what Carl had sent me last birthday. It made me wonder whether Carl had expected me to know that two bouquets of red roses were a symbol of something final and funereal. Maybe he had made a really obvious good-bye statement and I had totally fucked up by replying with an invitation to get together. Leave it to me to always do the wrong thing at the wrong time. Where was the definitive book on how to decode floral signals?

The next day was Mom's funeral. Because she had never exhibited religious inclinations of any kind, Dad decided to have someone from the wellness center run the service.

Wellness Woman was one of those artsy-looking middle-aged ladies in a peasant blouse and long Navajo Indian skirt who wore olive green orthopedic rawhide sandals with arch supports built into them. She had very, very thin, long white feet with unusually long, bony toes.

When she spoke about the woman she had met in the wellness group, I heard about a woman who was unlike the one who had called herself my mother.

This one was funny and glib and easy to talk to. This one had kept the wellness group enlivened with her wisecracks.

I was kind of sorry I hadn't met this version of her and yet in a way relieved. She would have been much easier to miss than it was to miss the one I knew. I would have been much sadder to hear about her passing.

I knew we had a troubled relationship. But I didn't know how troubled it was until I tried to participate in a "saying good-bye" exercise orchestrated by the thin-footed Wellness Woman.

We were asked to close our eyes and imagine a beautiful place. I saw a section of Tuolumne meadows, up near Yosemite, where I used to go camping when I was in college. The grass was long, vivid chartreuse, and dotted with wildflowers. I located myself at a picnic table in the middle of this idyllic landscape to await my mother's arrival.

And on cue, my mother appeared at the edge of the woods near the horizon, looking very businesslike and well groomed. She had on her lavender velveteen pantsuit with a matching silk scarf tied around her neck. Her hair was fluffy from being freshly bleached and blow-dried. Her makeup was perfect, her jewelry coordinated. She seemed competent, healthy, and in control as she trudged through the long grass toward me.

"This is where you bring me?" she said, shaking her head in irritation. "You gotta be kidding! You don't expect me to sit down at this filthy picnic table in what I'm wearing! And I am certainly not going to sit down in the meadow and get grass stains all over my brand-new pantsuit!"

At her wits' end, she turned and left the way she had come.

The most embarrassing part of the funeral was that I could not make myself cry. I wanted to cry. The women from the wellness center all cried. I tried to cry. My father, who never cries, cried. The women of the wellness center clearly viewed me as some kind of a monster.

I screwed up my face to get ready for a cry. The best I could do was to make myself really miserable.

For years I had worked so hard not to engage my mother's anger that I had lost a direct connection to her entirely. Now she was gone. The disconnection was all that remained. Turns out it's easier to fake orgasms than it is to fake tears.

I thought emotional problems like the ones we had somehow resolved themselves before your parents left the planet. I thought a tear-filled reconciliation was inevitable: a moment of tragic enlightenment like in *Terms of Endearment.* I assumed that proximity to the end of life forced a certain begrudging spiritual consciousness on a person.

It never occurred to me that my mother could just up and die in the same emotional muddle in which she lived.

The hole she left was a hole filled with unsolvable arguments and war strategies I would never have occasion to use again. Saying good-bye to those was nothing except a gigantic relief.

I actually believed for a brief shining moment that her absence might bring about a closer relationship with Dad. He might need me now. If she had been the troublemaker in the equation, he and I might have a chance to bond more deeply as he emerged a solo act.

But warning signs were already in the air the day of the funeral.

That afternoon it was decided that we (Dad, Evelyn, and I) would all go out to the coast and take a nice peaceful walk along the beach to contemplate our loss.

Since there was no such thing, in my father's world, as an afternoon activity, no matter how gut-wrenching, that did not involve a structured lunch, we stopped at a local market along the way to custom-order a couple of sandwiches.

It was kind of touching watching Dad bravely step up to the plate and assume the mantle of primary food critic. He opened with the observation that they used way too much mayonnaise. He only wanted half that much. On a piece of bread from the middle of the loaf. And thinly sliced onion. Don't you know what thinly sliced means? You don't really call that thinly sliced, do you? He was nearly as effective alone as the team of them had been.

By the time he got his sandwiches, the deli guy was muttering under his breath to everyone with whom he made eye contact about how some people were impossible to please.

We drove out the coast highway and we parked at the entrance to a flat, straight, mile-long trail. It was manicured, with tall, wheatlike grass growing on either side of a walking path made of packed dirt and sand.

From the moment we began, Dad was focused like a laser on Evelyn. At first I thought it was just his grief and nervous energy seeking release. Maybe I was making it all up. Then I began to wonder if maybe all Mom's fretting had been about something after all.

Never had I seen two people walk more slowly not just on a trail but anywhere, ever, than my father and Evelyn. They were tottering dangerously beneath the minimum definition of walking. To keep pace with them required performing the earthbound equivalent of treading water: a kind of subtler execution of the mime classic "Walking Against the Wind."

Finally frustrated by their almost total lack of forward movement, I decided to head down the trail by myself. I had part of a protein bar in my pocket. If it took them a couple of hours, I knew I could survive the wait.

When I arrived at the water's edge, some two or three minutes later, the sight that greeted me made me gasp. There, on a pristine section of coastline, framed by an aquamarine horizon, was the most remarkable panorama of wildlife I had ever seen outside of the pages of *National Geographic*. The entire area was covered with gigantic sea lions and their brand-new offspring. No zoo display was ever this lively or this populated. The beach was alive with playful baby animals, flinging themselves around in the sand, playing jolly sea lion games.

These were not just ordinary sea lions either. They were a much-larger-than-average variety—the big bulky kind that have longish hair and tusks and look kind of like David Crosby.

It was such an astonishing counterpoint to the funeral we had just been through that I was eager to share it with my mourning father.

Twenty-five minutes passed as I continued to patiently wait for the two of them to arrive—the slowest walkers in America doing God only knew what on the quarter of a mile they still had left when I saw them last. I felt confident that the physical properties of motion ensured that they would arrive sooner or later, no matter how little progress a single step provided. So I continued watching the animals frolic, like a privileged guest. But now I was checking my watch every few seconds and beginning to worry.

When half an hour had passed, I decided to head back down the trail to make sure everyone was all right.

I only had to go about fifty feet when I saw them, Dad and Evelyn, seated under a big, shady oak tree, eating their tuna sandwiches and chatting.

"We got hungry," Evelyn said. "We decided this was far enough."

"We knew if we sat here long enough you'd be back," said Dad. "What took you so long? Sit down and have a sandwich."

"You're only a few feet from the beach," I said. "You have to walk down there with me. There is the most gigantic colony of sea lions and baby pups only fifty feet from here. Maybe less. You gotta see it!"

Evelyn popped the last of her sandwich into her mouth, then began making the remaining Saran Wrap into a teeny, tiny ball.

"Seals. Yuck," she said. "I don't really care for seals."

"We're not into walking any farther," my father piped in. "If you want to go look at seals, go. Be my guest. Look at all the seals you want. But we're very happy sitting right here, thank you."

I was surprised by his abrupt tone. I guess I expected him to want to spend time with me, this soon after Mom's funeral. I thought we might find comfort in each other. But apparently not.

So I went back down to the beach alone and stayed there long after I was fed up with watching the seals myself, just to make a passive-aggressive point. A point, by the way, that was clearly lost on my father and Evelyn. They were still chatting with intensity under the tree fifty yards away when I rejoined them.

About an hour later, we all left.

Within the week, Evelyn and my father began seeing each other on a daily basis. And by the end of the month, they moved in together.

It was as if there had been no death. Everything was back in place for him as it had been before. Except now my mother wasn't around to worry that Dad had designs on Evelyn.

My father wanted continuity. My father got continuity. Evelyn was as close to a Mom replicant as he could have conjured, even through cloning.

Which brings me to today . . . my birthday, about six weeks later. This year I assumed the big celebration would involve the debut of Dad and Evelyn as a team. I was all ready to see how Evelyn ranked in the antagonize-the-waiter competition.

But much to my surprise, Dad came by himself. Apparently Evelyn had other obligations. Secretly, I was kind of pleased.

This was our first birthday alone together. I don't want to give the wrong impression when I say it felt a little like a date, but in a way it kind of did. I realized I had never had his undivided attention before. The idea of it made me kind of giddy. Maybe, just maybe, I was thinking, if I established a closer, more loving relationship with him on these new terms, it would have some kind of positive effect on my mysterious, never-ending relationship troubles with men. Maybe, like an allergy vaccine, the problems in our relationship contained the seeds of the cure.

I made reservations for eight o'clock at a chic, trendy place in Beverly Hills that I thought might impress him. It had all the things an important restaurant was supposed to have: big, expensive art pieces, waiters with fashionable haircuts in khaki pants, menu language full of overly elaborate descriptive phrases featuring unusual ingredients like tricolor mushrooms, or chipotle mayonnaise, tables full of showbiz regulars, all of whom might be Jeffrey Katzenberg. The explanations of the specials by the waiters when they came to the table were so lengthy and full of recipe particulars that it felt like a late-night infomercial for some kind of cookbook.

At 7:59 we walked in, looking all neatly ironed and cologned. That was one thing about Dad: very good hygiene. He had the kind of creases in his pants with which you could open an envelope.

By 8:05 when we hadn't been seated, my father's internal

clock apparently signaled that it was time for the fighting to begin. Looking back now, it's ridiculous that I didn't see it coming. But I honestly thought that maybe the fight-picking days would fade off now that the testier member of the team was gone: a thought that now seems as delusional a notion as expecting the violence to cease when Curly left the Three Stooges.

"We made a reservation for eight o'clock," Dad said to the *GQ* modeling hopeful who worked as the maître d'. His response not only to Dad's dilemma but to Dad's very existence indicated not only a complete absence of concern, but a crippling lack of available facial expressions.

"Perhaps you'd like to have a drink at the bar while you're waiting," he said to the empty space above our heads, as he scanned the edges of the room for more important faces.

This immediately turned my father's anger meter up a notch.

"I don't care to have a drink at the bar. I'd rather drink at the table. It is after eight, our reservation was for eight. I see empty tables all over the room. We'd like to be seated at one of those."

It was as if my mother had never died. She lived on in the behavior of her soul mate. He was channeling her perfectly.

Unless, and this had never occurred to me until now, she had actually been channeling him. Maybe somehow she got assigned the role of the bad cop in their never-ending game of Browbeat the Wait Staff.

"The hell if I'm going to be talked to like that," he muttered to the back of the *GQ* model, who had turned to greet a party of guests who looked more like studio heads than did my father. "Let's go sit down at one of those empty tables. Let him try to make us leave."

He began to lead me to one of the so-called empty tables, all of which were prominently decorated with a card that said RESERVED.

"Dad . . . ," I began, tentatively at first, overcome with embarrassment and the desire to become invisible. Being escorted from the premises of an impressive four-star restaurant by members of their security staff was not one of my birthday wishes. Was there any way to escape? I decided to test the waters, like my shrink was always suggesting.

"It's my birthday," I said, in a voice so soft and girlish that for a moment I thought I was Ann-Margret in an Elvis movie. "Would it be okay if I make a special request? Can we please not start my birthday celebration off this year with a big fight?"

I wanted to say "big, embarrassing fight" but I thought that throwing in descriptive modifiers might be like pouring oil onto the flames. I said it very meekly, trying to use the kind of charm-filled feminine voice that I'm told affects men positively. I have heard of women who talk policemen out of giving them traffic tickets in this way. Although I can't recall that it has ever worked for me.

Still, I did expect that playing the birthday card would buy me a little sympathy. I hoped he'd look at me like I was crazy, then shrug and grin and say, "Well, okay, sweetie. It *is* your *birthday.*" That's what someone else's father might have said. Maybe Ann-Margret's father in an Elvis movie.

"Don't you tell me what to do, young lady" is what he said instead, refusing to look at me, livid with disdain. "I can get very nasty with you," he said.

Suddenly I didn't know him at all. I felt like I was living in one of those moments where the child finds out her father is a hit man with the mob. It chilled me and caught me off base. Was he actually threatening me on my very birthday? Threatening me with what?

Was I now seeing him for the first time? Was there some kind of bottom of the riverbed layer of more extreme nastiness I had yet to see? Had he always been just like my mother, only worse? It had never occurred to me before that I had Siamese parents, joined at the anger.

"I'm going to the ladies' room," I said, thinking I'd buy some time to figure out how to react appropriately to such a jarring moment.

"Don't hurry back," he said as I headed off. What had I done to trigger such an enormous wellspring of rage? Or was I now to become the recipient of a special reserve that had previously been on tap only for my mother?

I sat in the ladies' room, pointlessly running a comb through my hair, reapplying mascara to spiky eyelashes that were too thick with mascara already, calculating how often birthday dinners with my parents had left me hiding out in ladies' rooms.

Someone had left the California Living section of the *L.A. Times* folded on the sink so I reread a portion of an article on bulimia. It was a rehash of a million other articles I had read about bulimia, but this time I found myself viewing it from a practical standpoint. If I was going to spend this much time hanging around ladies' rooms, it would be nice if the time could double as a weight-loss opportunity. Perhaps bulimia was something I ought to look into.

I sat for what seemed like a long time there, trying to shake the chill I had gotten from the cruel expression on my father's face.

Although there was a wide assortment of irritable facial expressions in my mental Dad file, this one was unusually cold. It was notably colder than the more common red-faced one that was triggered by the interrupting of one of his anal-retentive rituals. That one was usually accompanied by a kind of a swatting motion. Both were manifested when I made the mistake of trying to ask a question during the sacred packing of the car trunk before a trip. My father packed a car trunk like he was designing a new fuel uptake system for a lunar module. Every separate element was carefully wedged into a scientifically engineered location. If I dared try remove my suitcase after it had been inserted because I had forgotten to pack any socks, the red-faced expression with the swatting motion was the result.

No, tonight's expression was closer to his famous moray eel: eyes narrowed into an unsettling, emotion-free stare. The eel face he made out at the coast after the funeral, when I asked him to come look at the sea lions and inadvertently interrupted his bonding with Evelyn, had been cold. The one tonight was a good 50 percent colder.

One thing about ladies' rooms, they have their own special time warp. A typical ladies' room minute is exactly two hours of main dining room time.

Using that conversion scale, it was about six hours of main dining room time when I had composed myself enough to think about rejoining my birthday party.

As I headed back to the battlefield, slightly better groomed if a little bit overmascaraed, I saw that my father was now seated at one of the empty tables that were not available to us earlier. I don't know if he was exercising squatter's rights or if he got a table the regular way. But, no matter how he took title, a waiter was putting menus and a breadbasket down and filling up the water glasses. As always, my father had gotten what he wanted.

"I bet this isn't fresh Alaskan salmon" is all he said, examining the menu intently after I had been sitting there with him for several painful minutes of complete silence.

The rest of dinner was quiet. I didn't know what to say. I thought he owed me an apology. He thought I owed him one. Somewhere in the afterlife, my mother must have been proud to look down and see how well we were upholding our long-standing family tradition of the unfathomable, constantly owed apology.

We both ordered the salmon. I thought it was fine. Dad thought it tasted "fishy" and sent it back for an autopsy. That was another family tradition: complaining that fish tasted "fishy," as though the idea was to take a piece of fish and make it taste "chickeny" or "chocolaty" or like a porterhouse steak. After all these years, it's possible that no restaurant food tasted right to him until after he had sent it back at least once for repairs. Because when it came back from the kitchen the second time, garnished with someone's invisible shoe print, he ate without complaining.

After a couple of martinis, he got a little maudlin and began to talk about Mom.

"We had a good marriage, your mother and I. She was a good woman," he said, chewing his onion and spitting part of it back into the martini glass. "She had her own opinions. And she let them be known. When I met her that's what attracted me. The way she spoke her mind. Of course that turned out to be a real mixed blessing. But a good marriage involves a lot of give-and-take. As the years went by, I got better and better at learning to tune her out."

Lovely, I thought to myself. *Just what every woman wants. The chance to express heartfelt opinions to a tuned-out husband.*

"That was the problem *you* had with her," he said. "You should have taken a tip from dear old Dad. You could never learn to tune her out. You had to jump in there on every crazy thing she said."

"Maybe I was showing her more respect than you were," I sniped back. "I took the things she said seriously."

"You were showing her more respect?" he said, incredulous. "You gotta be kidding me. All you two did was fight. That's not respect in my book."

"Well, if you two had such a great marriage," I heard escape from my mouth, like irritable bees through a hole in a screen, "then why was Mom always angry? And why was she so fixated on you and Evelyn being together?"

I didn't mean to say it. I didn't want to say it. It had been a miserable enough birthday without opening old wounds. But he was making me so goddamn angry, first with his disrespect for me and now with his maudlin rewrite of history. It was too late to take it back. Maybe my need to stir things up with him was his genetic contribution to my character boomeranging back at him. Now I had once again played a role in ruining my own birthday.

Happy Birthday to me.

He looked up from his coffee and raised an eyebrow.

"Biggest mistake of my marriage," he said to me.

"What was?" I said, getting very still.

"When I asked your mother if she would mind if I had sex with Evelyn."

And just like in a bad movie, I dropped my fork. It hit the plate with a clank at just the right time. If I had taken a sip of water I would have sprayed it out of my mouth in surprise. I had no way to deal with this except the clichés of physical comedy.

"You're kidding me!" I said to him. "You didn't really *say* that to her? Not out loud? Not for real? Did you?"

"Like I said . . . biggest mistake of my marriage," he repeated, picking up his cup and blowing on his coffee before taking a sip.

"But *why* would you ever even *dream* of saying something like that to her? What did you expect her to say? 'Yes'? 'Go ahead'?"

"Well, you have to understand," he said, cutting himself an extremely tidy wedge of chocolate mousse pie and lifting it to his mouth. "She wasn't feeling well for the last few years. She had pretty much cut me off sexually. Hmm. This crust is stale."

"But you don't *ask* about something like that. Where in the world would you get the idea that Mom was a free-love advocate waiting to happen?" I said to him. "Were you being stupid or just mean and hostile?"

"That's enough out of you," he said, returning his complete attention to his pie and coffee and never looking up at me again.

We drove home in silence. My dreams for an all-new relationship with him now seemed as embarrassing and unrealistic as the ridiculous situation I had put myself in with Trevor.

Apparently I never had any idea who he was. He had covered his tracks effectively all these years. And his silence had served him. I had taken him for smarter.

Was this the template I was using when I picked men for relationships? Never examining their contents too hard because the idea of someone unknowable seemed safer, more familiar?

It's no easy task trying to understand someone who doesn't try to understand himself.

So summing up: worst birthday to date by a big stretch. How dumb was I to think that the ones with Mom were as bad as they could possibly get?

On the bright side, there was no inappropriate piece of women's clothing to try on. In fact, it turned out there wasn't a present at all. Dad just bought me flowers. A pretty mixed assortment in a big green glass vase with a card that said, "Happy Birthday Dad."

Of course they weren't the only flowers I got this year. Oh no. Apparently the forces that rule the universe felt I hadn't been mystified or punished sufficiently by puzzling floral arrangements for one birthday. When I arrived back at my house after dinner, sitting on the front porch were the annual Flowers of Anxiety and Mystery from Carl. Same card as always: Happy Birthday Carl. Except this year it seemed like such a silly caricature of the previous years that I was starting to wonder if maybe he was in on the joke. Could "Happy Birthday Carl" be an ironic statement of some sort having to do with the fact that year after year I never acknowledged *his* birthday? Maybe written in the spirit of those people who say "You're welcome" when you have forgotten to thank them?

To add the necessary note of confusion, this year's flowers were more spectacular than in previous years. This year there were quite a few orchids, and lilies and irises and delicate little pink buds I couldn't name. It was about twice the size of the bouquet purchased by Dad, a detail that was not lost on Dad. "That's a hundred-fifty-dollar arrangement, minimum," he harrumphed. "What's that idiot thinking, spending a hundred fifty bucks on an old girlfriend?"

I, of course, was wondering the same thing. I hadn't heard a peep from Carl since I sent the letter last year. So obviously the point was *not* to try and be back in touch. Unless he hadn't gotten the letter from last year. Had it gotten lost in the mail? Had the incident at the restaurant changed his mind about wanting to see me?

I guess it's possible that I overplayed my hand. That by being so direct with him, I kind of scared him off. He didn't really know what to say to me now, so he was sending flowers instead as sort of an all-purpose, wordless greeting? Clearly he still had feelings enough to need to make contact?

Or maybe things started taking off with that girl from the restaurant *after* he sent the flowers last year. But now they were coming apart again, hence the flowers this year?

Which still left me clueless about the appropriate reaction to have to my mixed assortment of lilies and orchids and irises *this* year. Laurel weighed in with the idea that lilies represented renewal and rebirth, like at Easter. No one had any particular idea what orchids meant except access to wads of disposable cash.

I looked up the symbolism on the Internet. And some of what I saw was a shock. Orchids meant "You will want for nothing with me," which certainly was not the way I remembered it. But irises meant "I need to see you soon. I have an urgent message to give you." Could this be true? Was it possible he had an urgent message? If he wanted me to call him, wouldn't he have said so on the card? He wouldn't have expected the presence of irises to convey this to me, would he?

I considered writing to inquire, but that seemed too dangerous. I certainly wasn't going to make myself vulnerable to another rebuff.

The upshot of the whole thing was that I found myself getting weepy again. The combination of how weird it had been with Dad at dinner, and now having no idea how to react to this seemingly beautiful, potentially emotional gesture from someone I used to love was making me dizzy.

The thing I did comprehend was how far off base I had been for years in my efforts to try to understand the significant men in my life. Where does it leave you when you realize your own dad is not only not who you thought he was, but worse, he appears to be stupider and meaner than you imagined?

And that the man you had the longest relationship with to date continues to be out of your sphere of understanding entirely. Maybe that's the message of this birthday. If I could figure this stuff out, maybe I could move on to some better set of relationships with the opposite sex?

RE: The damn flowers—I decided to send a polite but very brief note this time, a version of the kind of note he sends to me: "Thank you very much for the flowers." And then my name. As though the flowers had been a gift from me. Which is actually the only way to look at them that doesn't make me ambivalent and filled with unresolvable anxiety and sadness.

What I Learned This Year That I Need to Remember:

1. Let Mom off the hook for sole responsibility of the bad birthdays past as well as for every other kind of bad behavior. Apparently she and her soul mate were a kind of two-dummy ventriloquist act.
2. A checkered, goofy love life filled with tragedy and strife is *not* better than a long blank period. Whoever said it is better to have loved and lost than never to have loved at all did *not* mean repeatedly, exclusively, and after the age of thirty-five.
3. When you have never loved at all, at least you have enough attention span left to get some reading done.
4. Never continue trying to interact with someone who cannot define the word "soon."
5. Just because there is heat in a kiss does *not* mean there is anything else in that kiss besides *heat*. And you're a fucking idiot if you think it does.
6. Maybe the best thing to do with Dad is to just sit there and say nothing.

What I Learned About Quantum Physics This Year:

Apparently of my two parents, Dad has many more photons than did Mom. His totally unexpected behavior on this year's birthday was the Heisenberg uncertainty principle at its finest.

In the new physics book I was trying to read, it says that in relative motion there are different perceptions of distance and time. Apparently identical watches worn by two individuals in relative motion will tick at different rates. Maybe that explains what happened with Dad at the restaurant this year on my birthday. He was at eight o'clock. I was at three in the morning.

Other Stuff About the Cosmos:

Well, the Hubble telescope has informed us that there are fifty million galaxies in the universe, five times as many as previously thought. Two astronomers finally located half the missing mass of the universe. Which made me feel like a complete and total idiot since I had no idea at all that half of the universe was even missing.

The missing mass, it turns out, is made up of many unseen, burned-out stars. These are known as white dwarfs. (Maybe the reason they weren't found sooner is because most of them are working the overnight shift at poorly lit restaurants in Silver Lake.)

What I Want to Learn in the Coming Year:

Something about string theory. Something that is more substantial than me making bad jokes about string.

Birthday X

Okay, I almost don't want to talk about which birthday this is. In fact, I refuse to talk about it.

But at least having lived this long, I finally learned something: *not* to celebrate my birthday exclusively with any genetically similar aging adults who call themselves my family.

This year I had *two* birthday celebrations, both kind of pathetic. But one of them not riddled with insecurity and pain.

I'll start with the fun one. Laurel and Janey came over and we did a candle ritual from a book that Laurel got me called *Casting Spells for All Purposes*.

We opened with a ritual guaranteed to attract *love* into our lives in which we lit a pink candle by a vase full of pink roses. Then holding a conch shell that contained dried lavender and rose quartz, we chanted to the goddess Venus to join us with the power of the sun in order to manifest some love. It was seven o'clock at night. I hoped the sun was listening from the other side of the world.

"I release this with the power of the Universe and the power of my own dignity and say so be it. And so it is. And so it will and shall be," we intoned in dead seriousness.

That three educated women would stoop to magic spells could, I supposed, be construed as really a sad description of our lives. I prefer to see it as creative or playful, and not a frightening setback for me intellectually as I enter another decade of existence.

We were building up to a ritual to help clear away negativity. Maybe we should have done that ritual first because before we could really get going on our love manifesting, there was a knock on the door. And there they were. *The flowers.* The confusing goddamn flowers.

Unexplained. Adorned with the same card as always: Happy Birthday Carl.

This year it was an enormous behemoth Japanese arrangement. It contained orchids, tulips, lilacs, jasmine, and honeysuckle (which the florist's dictionary said meant "Dost thou love me?") along with bonsai stems, bamboo, some kind of fan-shaped things, and a number of amazing passionflowers.

"I wonder if the Japanese theme has any significance?" Laurel said. "It's got a kind of a peaceful, artistic feel. Kind of sensuous and romantic."

There were many ways I could think of to describe Carl. Sensuous and romantic would not have been two of them.

"What significance could a Japanese theme possibly have, except as a reminder of Pearl Harbor?" I asked.

"No significance," said Janey. "It's just a standard FTD catalogue flower arrangement. Florists get a big instruction book on how to custom-make them."

"I don't agree," Laurel persisted. "I think when he sends the flowers he is saying, 'Hey, we shared a lot together. Let's keep the friendship alive.'"

"There are a lot of passionflowers in this arrangement," I noted. "Do you think he knows he sent me a bouquet that's full of passionflowers? And if he does, do they mean he feels passion?"

Once again I was feeling really confused and exasperated.

By now we all had polished off a couple of glasses of wine. No one really wanted to sit and stare at candles and conch shells anymore.

"I think he is saying that he wants to leave the door open for more contact whenever it might be appropriate," said Janey. "He obviously still has strong feelings of some kind for you. There's no law that says he has to send you flowers."

"So you *do* think they are a request for more contact?" I asked. "He sends the flowers because he's hoping I will take the initiative and make him talk to me?"

"I think he must be thinking about you, or he wouldn't send them is all I am saying," said Laurel. "No one sends flowers to an old girlfriend five years after a breakup unless they have some kind of an ulterior motive."

"Do you want to call him? I think if you want to, the flowers are saying he'd be glad to hear from you," said Janey.

"Why doesn't he call *me*?" I asked her.

"He doesn't know if you want to hear from him. You didn't send *him* anything for his birthday, did you?" she replied.

The good news is that this year the flowers didn't make me cry. Perhaps I was just too busy manifesting love and light. Or maybe I was overflowing with photons and therefore more unpredictable. Whatever the reason, I put them on the dining-room table and we all went out to eat.

The weird thing is that at the sushi bar where we were drinking sake a few minutes later, three dead-drunk college kids sent a note on a napkin over to our table. "We love you" is what they scrawled with a ballpoint pen that only released ink every other letter so it looked more like "We ov ou."

Yes, they were disgustingly wasted, incoherent, thirty or forty pounds overweight each and several decades too young. But on the bright side, it appeared we had successfully manifested *something* with our chanting, flower staring, and conch shell holding. Okay, it was clearly the minimum definition of "love." But it was a start. Next time we just needed to make the chant a lot more specific.

After dinner I talked everyone into going to see a male strip show just because we'd never seen one and it was the only newspaper listing that looked remotely festive, the other choice being a reunion concert of the Original Monkees.

I was secretly hoping that maybe male strippers would be surprisingly more erotic than long-haired, middle-aged men singing "Pleasant Valley Sunday."

I had no idea of how little thought male strippers have apparently given the topic of turning on women. Their show was the *opposite* of sexy: stupid Greco-Roman costumes, weird, jerky, crablike dance movements to bad disco music. If there had ever been a strip show full of women this far off the erotic mark, they'd be booed right off the stage.

That was the birthday part one.

Part two involved Dad and Evelyn, at the Velvet Flounder, the same upscale restaurant chain he and Mom always insisted on. That I have never really liked the place at all didn't seem to influence their unilateral decision to once again make it the dinner location for my special day.

"I'm sure they have something on the menu you will enjoy," Dad said. After last year, I made the decision to go with the flow, no matter what he said. No more arguing with Dad, even if it meant extreme personal embarrassment. Better to sit quietly humiliated than to risk another stare-down from the moray eel.

This time, when he called the waiter over to dress him down about the spots on the silverware and the water glasses, I noticed that Evelyn was grimacing.

"Look at the face she makes at me," he said to me, nodding toward Evelyn. "What do you two beauties want me to do?" he said, shaking his head uncomprehendingly. "You ever hear of the Ebola virus? How do you think it's transmitted? If you want to get salmonetta, be my guest."

"It's the *tone* you take with everyone, Trent," Evelyn said quietly. "I wouldn't mind if you said it *nicely.* You don't have to talk to him like he's your inferior."

"If I said it nicely, do you think he would pay any attention?" he said. "Anyway, are you saying he's *not* my inferior? What is he, then? My superior?"

"How about your equal?" Evelyn offered.

"He's my *equal*? A fucking busboy at a chain restaurant? You're calling him my equal? What exactly are you trying to tell me?"

"Happy Birthday to me," I said.

If all of that wasn't festive enough, when he got up to use the men's room, Evelyn leaned over and confided in me that she was planning to leave him at the end of the month: a shockingly new kind of experience for Dad, who was under the impression that any older woman would willingly put up with any kind of bad behavior from any man. "Heck—she's lucky to have a man at all" is the way he endearingly described it during a particularly demoralizing sermon in which he tried to convince me to continue lowering my standards until I reeled in someone, anyone.

Evelyn leaned over to me. "You have to show support for your father right now," she said. "He is going to need you once I move out. This is going to be very difficult for him."

"Are you sure you have to go through with this?" I said, feeling I had a right to a totally self-serving emotional reaction as kind of a birthday present to myself.

"I can't take it anymore," Evelyn said. "All the anger. All the yelling. I spent the last seven years alone and sweetheart, let me tell you, I was very lonely. But one thing I was not lonely for was the yelling."

"What does he yell at you about?" I asked her, as if I didn't know.

"Everything," she said. "I went to the store yesterday and bought four potatoes. He thought we only needed two so he called me a fucking idiot. Then he misplaced his jacket. He was sure I hid it someplace weird. It was right where he left it in the trunk of his car. You'd think he'd remember what he had in that trunk. You know how nuts he gets packing that trunk. But by the time he found it, he had already called me crazy, called me a moron. By then, he was over it and couldn't figure out why I was mad."

I felt sorry for Evelyn. I also felt kind of sorry for my dad.

He was used to having someone to yell at who didn't question his right to do so. Someone who just returned the compliment by yelling back.

"Do you *have* to move out though?" I asked her. "Have you thought about going to couples' therapy?"

"I'm not going to any damn therapy," my father said, returning to the table in time to hear the end of my comment. "Enough of this therapy crap. Don't get me going on therapy."

We all sat in a thick silence while Dad made himself comfortable. And then he did my mother proud.

"A toast!" he said, hoisting his glass, and simultaneously inspecting it. "Look at this guy's idea of a clean glass. Here's to your fortieth birthday," he said. "Enjoy your forties. Your fifties are no fun."

I hadn't really given my forties all that much thought. I had been avoiding thinking about them. But now suddenly they were hanging like a noose just above my head.

Evelyn looked at me, smiled superficially, and resumed buttering a piece of French bread. Then she winked at Dad. He reached under the table and pulled out a large, elaborately wrapped box: the first present ever picked out for me by Evelyn.

I opened it nervously. And there it was in all its glory—an all-denim pantsuit, with a lovely gingham trim on the collars and the cuffs and a sequin-trimmed gingham dolphin on the pockets and on the back. It was an entirely different variety of hideous than my mother would have selected. *Hers* would have been made of stretch denim. This was a fake denim print.

"I can't wait to see how fantastic it looks on you," she said, smiling. That we were out at a restaurant where they couldn't force me into trying it on was perhaps the greatest birthday gift I could have been given.

A month and a half later Evelyn moved out. I actually begged her not to leave. Without her presence in the equation, I knew I would move back up to Designated Irritant. Even though it had been my original role growing up in the family, I really wasn't interested in reclaiming it. Growing older has taught me that if I'm going to be screamed at pointlessly by someone, I should at least think I am in love with them.

When Evelyn moved out, Dad decided it was time to get a new place all his own: his first bachelor pad, ever.

I agreed to go help him move out of the house he and Mom had shared for forty years. When I got there he had already begun sorting his lifetime of belongings into piles.

By the front door was an obstacle course of things meant for the Salvation Army. As I leaned over to examine it, it began to look eerily familiar. Then it dawned on me why. I was looking at every present I had ever purchased for either of my parents over the past thirty years.

There were presents meant for birthdays, Christmases, anniversaries, Mother's and Father's Days. They included oversized pricey art books full of museum-quality prints by impressionists and surrealists. Then there were the equally expensive nature books: *The Art of Nature, The Art of the Seashell.* There was also a wine-making kit, an art deco pitcher, several giant, scented, expensively molded but never-lit candles, all utterly untouched, unopened, sometimes still sitting in the original tissue paper. I had been as off base in my gift giving as my mother.

I ended up taking most of my gifts home with me. If only I had known that this would be how it would all wind up, I would have bought them both more Betsey Johnson outfits and dangly earrings.

"Maybe you want to go through your mother's things before I give them all away," my father offered.

Mom's clothes formed a jagged landscape over by the door to what used to be their room. A giant fjord of clothing I would never wear under any circumstances.

I stepped past Mount Mom and into the master bedroom. It felt weird and sacrilegious opening up her closet and looking through it. I could hear her voice, telling me not to make a mess of things.

I opened her big jewelry box cautiously. I had watched her handle the things inside it with loving care for years. Now, when I looked at them, I was embarrassed about how little I liked the individual pieces. I took a gaudy gold bracelet and a pearl necklace, more out of guilt and nostalgia and general respect for the memory of my mother than any desire to wear them. I felt it was incumbent upon me to take *something*.

Then I came to the weirdest souvenir of all. There in her closet, next to a last remaining stack of shirts folded so tidily they looked like origami, was a pile of diaries I never knew that she had kept. Obviously my father had not noticed them. They were sitting quietly, unopened, as she had left them.

I removed them from their secret nesting place almost breathlessly. Never have books made me more anxious. Not even blue books from freshly graded exams were as fraught with possibly devastating information.

I offered them to my father, who, to my surprise, casually waved them off.

"No, keep them if you want," he said. "What am I going to do with the damn things?" *Just more stuff to tune out,* I guess he was thinking.

So I put them in a shopping bag and loaded them onto the

front seat of the car, where they gave off a terrifying electrical energy as I drove.

When I got home, I sat and stared at them, afraid to open them up. I felt certain that they contained the key to my mother. Maybe they would be too painful to actually read, full of more intense specifics about her than I was ever really intended to know. Was I ready to hear pathetic, angry anecdotes about her relationship with my father? Or even more terrifying, the details of their sex life? Would I learn heartbreaking things about her childhood? What if she had been abused as a child, or even molested? Would she break my heart by discussing how frustrated and sad she felt all the time? Would she finally say why? What if she spelled out, in excruciating detail, how much pain our relationship gave her and learning these things gave me a lifetime of agonizing sadness and guilt? Maybe everything I had presupposed about our relationship was going to be altered. Maybe, just maybe, I shouldn't read these diaries at all.

I poured myself a glass of wine. No, I was going to read them. I had to know what she had really been like. I wanted explanations. I wanted to know what was really on her mind. So I began to read them very carefully, at first, taking in every word, willing to wait for as long as it took for the revelations to begin.

By page four I started to skip whole paragraphs, then whole pages.

What I found in those books was more of what I already knew. One thing about my mother: She was nothing if not consistent.

For example, April 3, 1986, she summed up a visit she made with my father to St. Mark's Square in Venice, Italy.

Everyone goes on and on about this St. Mark's Square. It's so beautiful, it's so very this and so very that. The truth is it is shockingly gaudy and overdone. Most of the city of Venice is laughably overdecorated. Leave it to the Italians to do things in such extreme bad taste that it almost becomes appealing in a ridiculous way. The whole place, for my money, is highly overrated. A real tourist trap designed to clean out your wallet.

How could I have ever expected to get her approval when the entire city of Venice, Italy, got flicked off like a booger?

Thailand, in 1983, didn't fare any better. The food was greasy. The menus were filthy. The waiters were rude, stupid, and unkempt. The entire country was a minefield designed to keep her and my father from enjoying the kind of meal to which they were so rightfully entitled. In fact, they had such unpleasant dining experiences in Thailand it's surprising that we never went there for my birthday.

There was an ongoing sameness to their travel adventures. Whole countries conspired against them.

In chapter one, my parents would show up with all good intentions and check into a hotel. Almost immediately they would find it sorely wanting. What choice did they have but to get their rooms changed when they discovered that the toilet/bed/heat didn't work at all? The new room would make them a little bit happier yet still not entirely happy because of all the hard work and inconvenience having to change rooms had caused.

Then they would take a short nap, followed by a stroll around the town filled with the joie de vivre for which they were so well known, only to find the merchandise for sale in the stores sadly lacking in excellent workmanship and shockingly overpriced. After a dinner that seemed inordinately expensive, just plain inedible, or, if they were lucky, both, they would head back to the room to turn in early.

The next day my father would wake up with a bad cold or a fever. My mother would figure out how to place a call to a doctor using her own special pidgin version of the local language. A doctor would come to the room and administer something that would make my father fall asleep. He would sleep for the next two days, which is possibly all he ever wanted from the vacation to begin with.

While he was sleeping, my mother would wander around the markets, probably frustrated at not being able to check for misspellings in an unfamiliar language as she catalogued the prices of food for sale in order to make a comparison with the prices back home. "Apples are ridiculously expensive in Paris," said one entry. "Walnuts are dirt cheap here," said another.

In Spain,

after el doctore prescribed an antibiotic for la grippe and charged us 600 pesetas, I went to a store and bought a slice of ham, some Swiss cheese, a bottle of beer for me and a Coke for him, a large bottle of water, some chicken bouillon cubes, some crackers, an orange, a banana, and the Spanish equivalent of a KitKat bar. I ate the cheese, ham, and beer, some potato chips I had left from lunch, and gulped a banana. Trent had a cup of chicken broth, which I made on my portable hot plate. By my calculations it cost exactly twice what I would have paid at Super Mart but only a quarter of what we would have paid in the hotel dining room. By the way, the Spanish version of KitKat bars are so bad that they're laughable.

I put the diaries on a shelf in my closet, next to my mother's jewelry, and never took them out again after that.

I guess it's been another weird year, all in all.

There was less in the romance department this year than in any year previous. It might have been my own fault. In the interest of progress, and not starting my fourth decade by making any of the same mistakes, I decided I had to change my destructive pattern with men. I wouldn't allow myself to be attracted to and seduced by angry people anymore, only to complain about being victimized by them.

I was reading a pop psychology book that Laurel bought for me called *Break Your Stupid Chains.* And it said that someone in my predicament—someone with a pattern that wasn't serving them well—needed to start to look beyond the people who automatically attracted them. In my case the angry people were the people who perpetrated the negative pattern. So I needed to try and date the kind of people who *didn't* attract me.

Laurel had already initiated the plan by starting to date Len, a manager of a discount drugstore where she shopped. He was so completely not the kind of guy either of us usually met that he was almost dazzling in his ordinariness. They seemed so enamored of each other that neither of them could speak a sentence that didn't include the word "honey" at least once.

"Does honey want the rest of my french fries?" Laurel would say.

"If honey doesn't want them, honey will take them," Len would reply.

That took some getting used to—but I guess the biggest adjustment for me was the first time I phoned Laurel and honey had to repeat every bit of our conversation to honey, so honey could participate in the conversation. Sometimes it's as difficult to deal with the new relationships of close friends as it is to have a new relationship yourself.

Even so, I was thrilled she was happy.

Although I have to admit that the few times we all had dinner together I found it difficult to pay attention when Len pontificated. I was slightly interested in how he decided on and decorated the seasonal displays for his store. But he also said a lot of things that sounded like he had memorized them from the *Farmer's Almanac*. Things like "Well, is everyone ready for Groundhog Day?"

Laurel claimed to find these things charming and comforting. I kept thinking that I much preferred a guy who had actual thoughts.

Meanwhile her happiness inspired me to give the date-a-guy-I-find-unattractive program a whirl in the name of instigating change.

It led to some of the all-time most confusing encounters with men I have ever had, complicated by the fact that I felt I wasn't allowed not to like them. I started out unattracted. Now it was my job to like them somehow, no matter what.

Enter Sonny, a guy I met at a party with the And-Michaels. Dawn (of Dawn and Michael) gave him quite a buildup. He was her sister-in-law's half brother. *Everyone* who met him love, love, loved him. He was the kind of guy women who say they want a great guy are all looking for, she told me.

I was primed to meet him. And, yes, it was *no* love at all at first sight. Which I decided to try to think of as a good sign.

He wasn't horrible-looking. No missing limbs or nightmar-
ishly bad proportions. He was reasonably fit, in reasonably
good health. He didn't have an obvious odor or a strange, distracting speech impediment.

It was really more his complete and total lack of energy that
was the problem: Like a human vacuum cleaner, he seemed to
suck all the energy out of me when I talked to him. He was pale
and slouchy in his big flannel shirt.

"I am so not attracted," the dumb girl whined.

"Perfect," I countered.

So I said yes to dinner with him later in the week. But I had
an attitude that was hard to shake. I not only drank heavily that
afternoon, I didn't make a special effort to buy new underwear
or shave my legs or pick out an outfit.

He won a few points for agreeing to stop by an art exhibit
that I'd been wanting to see at a gallery in Venice. But then lost
them immediately by making the comment, "My eight-year-
old nephew could have done these paintings." I could feel my
blood pressure rising, as it always does when my parents make
a comment about art that's this primitive.

"Yes," I replied, "but it didn't occur to your eight-year-old
nephew *to* do these paintings, now did it?"

Then I had to work hard to thaw the frost from my heart
before we arrived at the restaurant.

I became determined to find something about him with
which to bond.

He had a job that totally bored me. He was a webmaster for
an Internet site where people could trade duplicates in their
collections of whatever with each other. "I Already Have That
One.com" is what it was called. He regaled me with tales of

spoons that traded for fifteen but were really worth forty. I used the time to think up a really good new assignment: Using two-point perspective, put all the things that really bug you into a landscape. I couldn't wait to see what some of the kids came up with.

I made it to the third date, which involved going sailing on his medium-sized sailboat during a squall. I've never been too interested in sailing under the best of conditions. Sitting quietly, as a passenger, while someone else drives you around in circles has always seemed pretty much the definition of tedious to me. However, Sonny liked bad-weather sailing best because he felt it was more challenging. He only liked to take the boat out when there were small-craft warnings.

This side of him, his more macho side, featured him dressed in a yellow slicker swigging brandy straight from the bottle whenever a spray of water hit him, then singing portions of Irish sea chanties loudly to show his seaworthy character. In this incarnation he was a little more interesting than the dot-com goon because he saw himself as a kind of Ernest Hemingway figure. I worked as hard as I could to believe that he might actually be one. I actually tried making out with him in a last-ditch effort to build a little heat into the situation.

His kisses kind of felt like getting a sponge bath after gum surgery. I had never really kissed a guy who didn't attract me before. I assumed there'd be some way to get into it. But alas, there was no place to go. Ernest Hemingway would not have wanted his image dragged into kisses like these.

He finally lost me, once and for all, when he stood on the front of the boat and, wind whipping in his hair, insisted on reading me some of his poetry.

"When night fell, the sea came alive with smells, as though it had a thousand noses" was the line that pushed me past the point of no return.

Ultimately I had no choice but to conclude that when a date has put you in a mood that makes you think you'd rather be dead, this does not bode well for the development of a lasting relationship. Where falling in love is concerned, apparently no attraction is not enough.

Of course, the wildly mixed signals I'd been giving the poor guy completely blew his mind. He kept calling, wanting to get together. He couldn't fathom what the problem was since I had been acting so obviously attracted.

Which made me realize that for the first time I had ascended to the coveted position of asshole in this scenario. I guess this could be construed as progress. At least the dumb girl hadn't talked me into being the victim again. But to go from being the victim to being the asshole was not the kind of progress I was hoping to make. I had finally become one of the guys I was trying to stay away from.

Meanwhile, Laurel was out there, working the edge. She decided to marry Len, her discount drugstore manager honey, in a wedding that was eccentric, even for her. Because it was her second marriage in a relatively short period of time, she and Len decided they didn't want to spend a lot of money. This time she did want to invite some friends, so Len came up with the idea of having her wedding double as a charity fund-raiser. That way they could make a lifetime commitment, a philanthropic statement, and at the same time have a handsome tax write-off.

Instead of gifts, they asked for donations to the American Lung Association since both of their fathers had died a few years before of lung cancer. Then Len took the whole thing a step farther by somehow using his drugstore connections to talk the Philip Morris Company into underwriting the cost of the reception in exchange for sending publicity releases to the local media outlets.

"I know it seems weird, but this is actually really ground-breaking," Laurel said to me. "A big cigarette company and the American Lung Association working hand in hand. Len was so smart to think of it. They are also donating a nice little gift bag of smoker's accessories . . . like a cigar cutter and a T-shirt and a cap and a copy of *Cigar Smoker's* magazine, that I can give out as party favors to all of my guests."

It was one of the strangest weddings I ever attended, fol-lowed by one of the most bizarre parties. Sentimental photos and traditional wedding buffet foods mingling beneath ban-ners for Philip Morris and the American Lung Association.

I decided it was not in my best interest to interact too much with Laurel about her wedding choices. I just hoped she would be happy with Len, that he would turn out to be less nuts than the Internet Boy, that he wouldn't hang up on me when I called, and, if it did work out, that I would really get a discount on seasonal decorations and office supplies at his store like he sort of hinted one night at dinner. Making a marriage work is clearly not as easy as I once thought. Who's to say that a big fat check to the American Lung Association and a free gift bag of smoker's accessories for the guests wouldn't be of some karmic help?

One thing I have learned: There is no accounting for the love choices of your friends. As long as "honey" seems to be happy with "honey," it behooves one to just play along cheer-fully and accept who- or whatever each individual "honey" might drag in. Kind of the way you do when your cat leaves a rodent or a frog corpse in the living room on the couch.

Which brings me back to Carl and the damn flowers. After all that stuff Janey and Laurel fed me on my birthday about the flowers being a gesture intended to open the door for communication, I started to think that maybe they were right.

Our relationship ended because I thought he was an asshole. He was lying. He was cheating. He was mean to me.

But then again I wasn't all that evolved as a person back when we lived together. Some of my behavior was needy and adolescent. Maybe I had been an asshole and coconspirator in the carnage myself.

Maybe I hadn't been as understanding of his insecurities as I could be now. I hadn't been to therapy. I hadn't read fifty thousand psychology books yet. Maybe if he and I met again on a neutral ground, things could be vastly improved. I started thinking about how way back at the beginning, when we first met, things had been really fun. We used to have all kinds of chemistry. We used to go places and laugh until my mascara ran down my face and he would make raccoon jokes about me.

Maybe, I was thinking, if I initiated a renewal of the friendship part, something good would come of everything in general. There had to be some reason he was still making contact with me on my birthday, four years later.

So I spent two days constructing a message to leave on his answering machine that would be poignant and caring, yet detached enough not to be intimidating or have any kind of a treacherous, manipulative feel.

After making several drafts of my sentiments, I dialed his number, knowing I would hang up if I didn't get the machine.

"Hi," I said with great relief, when I did. "It's me. Just calling to say thank you. It means a lot to me that you still remember my birthday. And if you're ever in the neighborhood and want to go have some coffee or any other hot beverage or cold beverage or even a room-temperature beverage—I'm still at the same number. So feel free to call."

He called back once two days later and left a very noncommittal reply.

"Hi, this is Carl," he said. "Are you there? No. Okay. Well, this is Carl returning your call. Hope you're well." Then he hung up.

His voice didn't sound especially interested, though it had no traces of hostility. If anything, he sounded distracted.

I called him back again and this time I left an equally noncommittal reply. "Hi, it's me again," I said. "Just calling you back. Hope everything is good."

The next time he returned the call, a day later, it was via his assistant.

"Carl Kerwin returning" is all she said.

I never heard back from him again. I gave up and I guess so did he.

What I Learned This Year:

1. I know last year I said I would give up all mumbo jumbo but sometimes a little mumbo jumbo can inject a note of hope in a situation where it all seems hopeless. In the future if I am going to mess with mumbo jumbo I have to word all magic spells very carefully. The word "love" is not sufficient. Next time I need to remember to add modifiers like "appropriate," "reasonable," "appealing," and "*hot*."

2. Don't expect Dad to appreciate or approve of anything I ever do. Just accept him for who he is, whoever that is. And deal with him accordingly.

3. Realize Mom was exactly the person she appeared to be. And I will never have an explanation for it. So forgive her. She lived in the dark. She died in the dark. She did the best she could in the dark.

4. If it has to get down to dating people who do not attract me, it's probably better to just not date at all. Staying home alone does not deprive a girl of the will to live.

5. Which brings me to the big question: Have I fallen into the Hole? And if I have, will I now be in here *forever*?

   I don't know how to look at this. If I say I am in the Hole, it will indicate that I have given up hope. I have often heard it said that the thing you want appears when you least expect it, after you have totally given up hope.

   But, deep in my heart, I can sense that I have not really given up hope.

   Which makes me wonder if my allowing hope to live is what is clogging up the plumbing. On the one hand, I think that maybe if I start to admit that "Yes. I am in the Hole. I have finally given up hope," then that very admission will speed up the process of sending a healthy relationship my way. And on the other hand, I worry that the very act of forcing myself to prematurely give up hope in the name of speeding things up is in fact an act of hope.

   Either way I wind up screwed.

What I Learned About String Theory:

Inside the smallest particles of the universe are vibrating, oscillating, eleven-dimensional strings. Eleven dimensions is about nine dimensions more than I can imagine since even three dimensions has always seemed a little excessive to me. And now, apparently, the idea of three dimensions is totally obsolete. I don't know if all those additional dimensions will maybe increase my chances of finding love, but I have a feeling that when we figure out where they all are, I already have loose papers and unopened mail piled up in eight of them.

That's not even the weirdest part. According to someone named Stromlinger, "the notion of space-time which we have cherished for thousands of years is clearly something we are going to have to give up." At first this made me sad. And then I thought, *Good riddance. I have never been good at managing either one of them.*

According to string theory there is no clear difference between now and the instant *after* now, e.g., "So how can we say whether the gunshot caused the death or the death caused the gunshot?" *This* idea is definitely good news for fans of Court TV. Because if it ever makes its way into our legal thinking, the next O.J. trial will definitely go on for several decades.

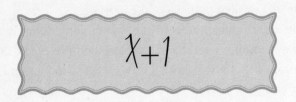

X+1

I DECIDED TO TAKE a completely different route into the birthday mess this year by spending my damn birthday alone. No more potentially inflammatory situations. Go the peaceful, serene route. Let the aging process proceed without any particular resistance, cooperation, or pretend celebration from me.

But at eight A.M. before I could even decide what course of action I was planning to take, the doorbell rang and there they were again: the Fucking Flowers. A big all-white assortment this year: White orchids. White roses. White lilies ("purity and beauty"). White flox ("appreciation"). White tulips. White, white, white. In a white ceramic vase.

He did it again, I thought. *Why white? Does that mean a truce? That's what white means, right?*

"Obviously," said Janey, "you really have to sit down with him and talk."

"I wrote to him one year. I called him one year. He never responds," I said.

"He's always been a cryptic, nonverbal kind of guy," said

Janey. "I know a lot of corporate guys like that. You're right. White does mean 'truce.' Or 'peace.' It's too symbolic a choice *not* to have a meaning."

"But what does it mean in terms of Carl and me at this point?" I said. "Is this symbolic of an ending or a beginning?"

"I guess you wait and see," she said. "At the minimum, I think he's saying he wants your friendship, your approval."

The fugue of confusion that descended this year after the flowers arrived made me more eager than ever to have this be a year in which I became a more clearheaded me. As a first step toward that greater clarity, I decided that my birthday, a day of new beginnings, was as good a day as any to fire Lolanna. It seemed like a good business decision. She had been shrinking my clothes and breaking my dishes with such regularity that not only could I really not afford to keep her based on damages alone, it almost seemed like she was begging to be fired. Plus now that Mom was gone, my cleaning style had ceased to be so controversial. Dad rarely came over.

But I found the idea of firing Lolanna so unsettling that it literally made me sick to my stomach. I paced. I took Pepto-Bismol, then rehearsed a short speech in which I claimed that I, too, had just been fired. Then I took more Pepto-Bismol and considered just leaving her a letter and an envelope stuffed with a generous amount of severance pay. However, I was pretty sure she couldn't read.

When she finally showed up for work, she had two nursery school–aged children with her: a little boy, about five, in a tiny Dodgers cap and a little girl, about four, in a pretty pastel dress carrying a stuffed Barney. She looked so cute with them that the new, clearheaded me not only didn't fire her, I gave her forty extra dollars for no reason. Then I left to run errands since listening to two preschool-aged children yell at each other in Spanish was not my idea of the way I wanted to spend my birthday.

On my way out the door, Dad called wanting to make birthday plans.

We really hadn't been getting along for a while now, since he did indeed bump me up to Designated Irritant. Using me to vent his anger had become a hobby to him, not unlike crossword puzzles or golf.

Nevertheless, I didn't have the courage to say I wouldn't see him. I agreed to meet him at the restaurant of his choice later.

Then I avoided the event for as long as possible. I spent the day buying three new tires at a discount tire place. And as if that wasn't birthday excitement enough, while they were being rotated I went into a sushi bar across the street and drank sake. This made me feel so pathetically sorry for myself that I realized I could never exercise the "spend my damn birthday alone" option again.

It's a good thing I drank plenty of sake, though. Because when I finally met up with Dad a couple of hours later, at a steak house he insisted on despite the fact that I haven't eaten red meat in fourteen years, he had a date with him. A date who was six years younger than I am. She was a mousy-looking girl with a Texas accent, dressed in clothes that made her look like she was attending a costume party as a member of my father's generation, a Gen-X version of a fiftyish accounts receivable clerk. Everything about her seemed very middle-aged except the unlined pinkness of her skin. She looked like a teenager wearing too much makeup.

"This is Anna Louise," said my father.

To say that I was shocked is to understate.

"Happy Birthday!" said Anna Louise with more intimacy and warmth than a person who had never laid eyes on me before was entitled to have. "It's so nice to meet you at last. Your father has told me a lot about you."

"He has?" I said. "How long have you two known each other?"

"We met at my art class," my father piped up.

"When did you start taking an art class?" I asked.

"About a month ago," they both answered at once, then looked at each other and giggled as though they couldn't get over how in tune they were. Chills ran up my spine.

When I sat down at the table, I was afraid I would shatter glassware with the sheer force field of my attitude. I simply didn't know what to do with this situation. I also quickly fixated on the fact that Anna Louise was playing my father like a violin. She even acted charmed when he explained to her his complex methodology for putting a napkin in her lap.

"Put one end of the napkin in each hand and shake it out like this," he said to her. "See how I shake it so it unfolds completely? This way it covers more of the lap area."

"Hmm!" she said. "I don't think I ever really get it completely unfolded all the way. That's a very good point. This will make a big difference."

My father smiled, proud to be acknowledged at last as the master of all specific details: napkin expert extraordinaire.

Watching her face, I felt like someone was pouring cold water down my back. It was incredibly frightening to see her successfully manipulating my naïve, egomaniacal father. "I learn a lot from your father," she said to me. "He has so much good advice."

"If you're blown away by his napkin techniques, wait until you see how effortlessly he makes his own breakfast," I muttered.

After that I refused to look her in the eyes again for the rest of the meal. However, as the evening went on I wanted to strangle my father. It was embarrassing to see him act so transparently uncomprehending. The way he was buying her trumped-up adulation as genuine affection made me realize he didn't know what real affection looked like any more than I did. Unlike me, he had the confidence and arrogance to expect people to love him just because he showed up. He was like a constantly petted, overconfident golden retriever. By comparison, I felt like I had been raised at the pound in a cage that said I had forty-eight hours to live.

I don't know why I was surprised. For forty years he and my mother behaved as though extreme irritation was the face that people who loved each other wore. Why in the world would it suddenly occur to him to be suspicious of overblown fawning?

The conversation we had at dinner totally drove me up a wall. Suddenly my father was asking me questions as though he'd only known me for a few weeks.

"How is your health?" he asked me. I couldn't recall him asking me that question ever before.

"How is my health?" I asked. "My health is just fine. How is your health?"

"I've never felt better," he beamed, and reached over and took Anna Louise's hand.

"Do you take vitamins?" Anna Louise asked me. "I'm a big believer in vitamins. I take about ten different ones every day."

"I don't really care about that kind of thing," I lied, deciding not to mention that I take about fifteen vitamins a day. I didn't want to agree with her about anything.

"Oh, you really should," she said. "As we get on in years, it's important to make sure all the nutritional needs of our bodies are being met. You should at least take a multivitamin, E, and calcium. None of us get enough calcium. I just bought some for your dad."

"She's got me taking vitamins! How do you like that?" he beamed.

"Whatever," I said, looking into the middle distance and then feeling sick because I was acting like my mother. I don't know why this pushed my buttons so hard. I guess because I thought I heard a slightly patronizing tone in Anna Louise's voice, as though she and my father were the adults and I was the child. And maybe also because I had recommended thousands of times to my father that he take vitamins but when I said it he always turned a deaf ear.

By now I was time traveling into a hideous future that the three of us would inhabit. I was imagining having to spend vacations and holidays with the two of them. I would have to buy her Christmas gifts and birthday presents and pretend to be glad to see her. I was imagining my father changing his will to leave everything he owned to her. I hated her guts.

Even more specifically annoying, I could see she already had more power over my father than I had achieved in forty-one years.

"You should listen when someone gives you good advice,"

my father chimed in. "Anyone can see how well the vitamins work. Anna Louise is a beautiful woman. Take a look at what a great figure she has!"

"So, in other words, you're saying that, by comparison, I don't really look that great?" I asked him.

"See how she twists my words around," my father said. "Did you hear me say that, Anna?"

"No. Not at all. Your father was just giving me a compliment," she said. "He didn't mean to imply anything negative about you."

Can I just go home now? is what I was thinking. "Gee, is it nine already?" is what I said.

"By the way, vitamins don't have any effect on your figure," I sniped, with more dismissive irritation than it really merited. "Did it occur to you that maybe Anna Louise's fantastic figure comes from her having inherited the right genes from some really good-looking parents?"

For a minute or two, I felt a tiny bit proud because this pointlessly mean-spirited rebuke represented a certain kind of progress. It was the first birthday fiasco initiated solely by *me*. That was when I realized I better get out of there immediately because this was rapidly turning into the point in the birthday celebration where I would have to retreat for a minivacation in the ladies' room.

"I'm taking off," I said, putting on my sweater. "This has been a lovely little get-together. But I'm tired and I think I better head home."

"You can't leave now," my father said. "I ordered a special birthday cake and champagne."

"You haven't opened your present yet!" Anna Louise said,

looking right at me with so much false empathy it made my skin crawl.

I sighed and sat back down. The more I thought about it, the more curious I became. What would a woman six years my junior who was hell-bent on trying to reel in my father contribute to the hall of horrible presents?

So I took off my sweater, leaned back in my chair, and sat quietly through a fight Dad picked with the pockmarked twenty-four-year-old waiter about whether the mesquite grilled chicken was really free-range. Anna Louise acted like she appreciated the way Dad was looking out for her nutritional best interests. Neither of them noticed that the poor, demoralized waiter with the face full of broken capillaries looked like he might be on the verge of throwing himself onto the mesquite grill.

I sighed and played with the olive in my martini as Dad ran through all of his stories about being in the army, to a spellbound blond audience of one who was hearing them for the first time. Judging from her expressions, I think this might have been the first she had heard of World War II. Naturally she was rather alarmed.

The most difficult thing was figuring out how to react to Anna Louise as she tried out different tones of voice and approaches to use on me. It was as though she was figuring out how she was going to position herself when she became my stepmom.

And then there was the birthday toast. But first there was the cake. Dad ordered his favorite—chocolate mud pie—and to make it as joyous an occasion as possible, he asked the restaurant to put forty-one separate white candles in it surrounding the largest wax forty-one I had ever seen. It had to have been designed by the engineers at Disney. It was only slightly smaller than the HOLLYWOOD sign, just to make sure that everyone in the restaurant who hadn't thought I looked particularly pathetic before now looked over at me with barely concealed sympathy for a life tragically misspent.

"It wasn't so easy to find a candle that said forty-one," he only half joked. "I had to ask the party store to make it special from two single candles."

But ah, the toast! My mother was gone. My father could do his worst and I was ready, I thought. We all raised our glasses. I held my breath.

"To my daughter on her birthday," said my father. "Whew. I can't believe how old you're getting!"

I swallowed. Bad, yes, but I could adjust. I had been through worse. I was well into recovery when Anna Louise interrupted.

"May I offer a toast, too?" she asked.

"Yes, of course," said my father, before I could interrupt with "No. You don't even know me. Go away."

"Here's to a wonderful year. Even though you are probably thinking to yourself, 'Forty-one is kind of really getting up there,' " she said, with a sweet smile. "I mean, I don't know if that's what you're thinking but it sure is what I would be thinking, hon! But, you have to remember, it really is only a number and you are only as old as you feel. I have an aunt who just turned fifty-four and she said she has never felt better. So enjoy!"

"Nice toast," I said, starting to stand up and put on my sweater. "Catchy. You might want to submit that to toast-masters. Nice meeting you, Anna Louise. Enjoy the explicit instructions on how to button your coat."

Which is when Anna reached under the table and pulled out a big gift-wrapped box.

"Happy Birthday from both of us," she said, as though she did this every year.

"I couldn't have picked it out without Anna's help," said my father, who had only known me forty-one years.

I took the gift and ripped it open, defiling that wrapping paper as though I had never been repeatedly instructed about how to do it differently. And there it was, all neatly folded: A fake-leopard/zebra/tiger-skin ensemble. It wasn't my taste. I would never have bought it for myself even in a state of extreme inebriation. But unlike the outfits selected by my mother and Evelyn, Anna Louise was off in a way that I found totally intriguing. She had picked out a clingy-looking, stretchy, fake-animal-print-skin, long-sleeved sweater and a pair of matching black latex pants with an animal-print-skin trim. They were slutty-looking, like something Jayne Mansfield would have worn. Or Christina Aguilera. Or Dennis Rodman. The outfit lay there in the box, like a dare. I couldn't wait to try it on in private. This was a first, a brand-new birthday sensation. Dad's Gen-Xer girlfriend had much more intriguing bad taste than any of his previous romantic liaisons.

"Thank you," I said to them both, as I tried to decide if I should rethink my feelings about Anna Louise solely on the basis of her nearly acceptable birthday present.

"I think that'll look really rad on you," she said.

A few minutes later, when she got up to go to the ladies' room, my father leaned over and began to confide in me.

"I know she's a little bit of an airhead," he said to me. "But it's the best sex I've ever had. And I need that. I'm a very sexual guy. The older broads just can't keep up with me."

This was way, way too much information. I had been spared this side of him for the previous forty-one years, and whatever the reason, I was grateful.

"Your mother was the great love of my life," he went on, "but to be honest with you, she wasn't that good in bed. Never really into sex as much as . . ."

"That's enough Dad," I said. "Some things are best left undiscussed."

"Gee, I didn't realize you were so uptight," he said. "I thought I could talk about things with you."

"No, you really can't," I said. "I am much too uptight."

By now he was losing interest in me anyway because Anna Louise was visible at the far side of the room. As she began a slow sashay back to the table, the guy at the piano bar began to play "Close to You." Watching her walk toward him made my father beam.

" 'Why do birds suddenly appear, every time you are near?' " he sang. " 'Just like me, they long to be close to you.' "

It was a frightening moment. And not just because the whole idea of Anna Louise causing birds to suddenly appear for no real reason made me feel like I was living in the opening sequence of a horror movie. Add to that the notion of having to watch my father serenading a strange woman half his age with a love song . . . well, let's just say I would rather not have witnessed it.

"So! Thank you both for the lovely birthday," I said with a certain amount of actual honesty. "I'm going right home and try my birthday outfit on."

"You and Anna Louise should go out for lunch . . . spend a little time together," my father said to me. "She knows a lot about how to treat a man. You could learn a few things. She's not uptight at all."

The amount of time it took me to put on my sweater, leave the restaurant, enter my car, and pull out of the parking lot set a new international land record for speed.

When I got home, the first thing I did was try on my new trollop duds. Like a brand-new, really perfect Halloween costume, I never wanted to take it off, even to sleep. Well, to be honest, it was the second thing I did. The first thing I did was drink a large water glass of sake in one gulp.

Then I put on the radio and practiced prancing around, doing moves I would never do in front of actual people. I was Salt-N-Pepa, Queen Latifah, and Snoop Dogg's most beloved protégée. I had the grooves, I had the moves, and I was even getting good at that separated-fingers hand-gesture thing when I hip-hopped past the dining room, and the sight of the goddamn flowers quieted me down again. What *was* the deal on them anyway? What kind of response was he expecting from me at this point?

Perhaps a brief, positive thought, followed by no real contemplation. That was basically all that was required during the relationship. His questions were always rhetorical. The correct approach to getting along with him was really to agree with everything he said, without giving the appearance of agreeing with everything he said. He claimed to hate people who pandered to him. But he hated people who disagreed. He was such a contrarian that to get him to make love to me, I would have to lie next to him thinking, *I hate you. Don't touch me.*

We never once in all the years I knew him had sex with the TV off. It was such a consistent detail that the memory of the best orgasm I ever had with him included a dialogue run from a TV movie in which a woman has to go to Uzbekistan to search for her missing son. It went, "Oooh, yes baby, yes, tell me mister please, have you seen the young boy in this photo?"

Remembering these things was how I finally decided that the best thing I could do was say nothing about the flowers. If he wanted to talk to me, he'd find an excuse and make it happen. If I wanted to talk to him, the best thing I could do was ignore him.

I hip-hopped out of the room, wondering if it would have made any significant difference to our relationship if Carl had seen me dance in this slutty outfit.

Then I made another birthday vow. This would definitely be the year when I would stop picking guys who acted like my parents. The trouble was that I had a hard time telling who they were until it was too late. Having to comprehend that an adorable, brooding, sad-eyed guy in a leather jacket was my mother in drag could be very damn confusing.

I'd failed with guys who *didn't* attract me. I'd failed with guys who *did* attract me. What was left? Apparently the answer was Mike.

I met him four months ago at Borders Books the first evening that I ever tried wearing my birthday outfit out in public. I was so ill at ease wearing it, I couldn't look up at anyone. But he was standing right beside me at the New Fiction table. We were both opening and closing the covers of the new best-sellers.

I thought he had a nice intensity about him right away. He was wearing black jeans and an NPR T-shirt, which seemed a little pretentious but I decided not to eliminate him on superficial details too quickly. Especially since I was dressed in an unidentifiable fake animal skin. And despite the fact that I have noticed on many occasions that a person's superficial details can tell the whole story.

"This Martin Amis book is getting great reviews," he said. "Look at this picture of him. What's he got to look so grouchy about?"

"Well, I read he had some kind of dental surgery. That'll sour even a cheery person, which he probably isn't because he writes for a living. Somewhere along the line he and his father probably had a conversation about surly jacket photos appearing more profound," I replied.

"You could be right," he said. "Plus also, maybe he knows that even though we both read his great reviews, neither one of us is going to buy his book until it's out in paperback."

We stood there chatting with each other until I was ready to buy some books and leave. I wasn't planning to buy anything. But once I decided he was cute, I thought it made me look better to purchase a little new fiction. So I bought a short-story collection.

As we walked to the cashier together, I learned he was a high school English teacher.

"I guess I should get your phone number," he said.

"I guess you should," I said, considering giving him a fake one because I was paranoid about meeting a complete stranger.

"Maybe he's not who he says he is," the dumb girl was saying. "Maybe he's a serial killer."

But then I thought, *No one creating a false identity claims to be a high school English teacher. Not when you have the complete option of being something more exotic.*

So I rose to the occasion. I gave him my real number. And then I drove home, lost in a cloud of nervous tension and hormones.

He was kind of hot, I thought as I drove. Which meant I shouldn't agree to go out with him right away. I should drag things along for a while to make myself appear more intriguing. This would make him want me more. All the new books said that if you went for a guy too quickly, they would not want a real relationship with you. Although obviously if you dragged them along endlessly, they would not want one either. The key to success seemed to be to project just the right amount of reluctant agreement that would make him worried and yet hopeful at the same time.

Of course, he didn't call for almost five days. Not until I was starting to deliver lengthy speeches to myself about how I didn't give a fuck about him. As soon as I had totally given up all hope of hearing from him, just like they say . . . there he was, sounding totally appealing on my answering machine.

I was going to wait a couple of days before I called him back, but a couple of hours is all I could stand. He sounded glad to hear from me. We decided to go to a movie the next night.

When we hung up, I completely freaked. It had been *forever* since I had gone out with a guy who actually seemed interesting. I was way too excited.

I decided that there would be no sex. I had read all the books, listened hard to all the radio shrinks who said you shouldn't even consider having sex until there was a mutually agreed-upon feeling of love and a statement of commitment.

I knew all of this but I bought new underwear and a disposable douche, got a manicure, a pedicure, a haircut, and a bikini wax anyway. No reason not to play both ends against the middle. I was exfoliated, buffed and beveled to a high gloss, then oiled and cream-conditioned into a vanity-driven stupor. I was groomed so hard I felt embarrassed for myself.

After putting that much work into it, I felt the date would definitely be a disaster. But immediately we had that kind of great connection I love where we both just talk and talk and time flies by.

We went to a bar and had martinis so large they looked like props from *Lost in Space.* Then we played a round of miniature golf at a place down the street, where we were pretty much the only people on the course over ten years old. I laughed so hard that giant mascara tracks dripped down my cheeks. When I got a glimpse of myself in the handle of my golf club, I looked like a goth girl on her way to Ozzfest.

Afterward we went to dinner and talked some more.

It was almost a painful amount of fun. By the time we said good night, the dumb girl was all pumped up and lecturing me about the benefits of going to bed with someone right away.

"You should just go for it," she was saying. "You really don't know how much longer he'll be around. Or how much longer you'll be around, for that matter."

"But how much do I really know about him?" I answered, knowing full well she never slowed down enough to consider reading a résumé. "Yes, he was a good kisser," I continued, sensibly. "But the new clearheaded me knows better than to sleep with him based only on that, no matter how much you keep working on me."

"I had a lovely time," I said to him, pulling away. "Thank you so much. I hope we'll see each other again soon."

And then I drove home, my brain vibrating like a washing

machine on the spin cycle, as it dispensed endless insecure second guesses about how he felt about me.

"Yes definitely" is what I recall hearing him say. I'm pretty sure he said it. I don't think I made it up.

And then he didn't call me for three days, which seems like a really long time when you are mesmerized by hormonal snake-charmer music.

The three-day lull gave me a lot of time to pep-talk myself about taking better care of myself. I really didn't want to intentionally hurt myself again.

"Normal everyday life provides us with all the misery we will ever need," I said to myself. "It is *our* job to try to hold the misery at bay and to maximize the joy. Or whatever kind of lull from misery looks enough like joy to pass.

"Remember, it is better never to have loved at all than just get loved for a couple of days and spend the next few months boring your friends with the details, asking them over and over what they think he really meant when he left some weird answering-machine message," I reminded myself. Even though my hormones and the dumb girl were howling, "Go find him and climb into his bed and be waiting for him when he gets home!"

The good news was that I was conducting a real, two-sided debate. Okay, yes, both sides were *me*. But this seemed like some kind of progress, even if I was talking to myself.

"What kind of track record does he have in love?" my smarter, more clearheaded self was wondering. "Is he a good risk or a bad risk?" No one in my unit had any answer. We had no friends in common. There was no one I could ask. I typed his name into a search engine but nothing, not a single thing, came up. Except a boat rental place that had his last name as a first name. And an omelette parlor that had no names in common with him or the boat rental.

It seemed wrong that there was no website listing all his past liaisons that I could check. I wanted to read a few letters of recommendation. When you buy a used car, you have it inspected by a mechanic. Shouldn't there be a similar service for humans?

So I started to devise a plan. I would somehow locate a few of his previous girlfriends and talk to them long enough to develop a picture of what I was getting into exactly. One thing about ex-girlfriends that I definitely knew: If they were unhappy, they would tell you the truth.

"Why don't you just flat out ask him these questions yourself?" said the dumb girl, hoping for a solution that would satisfy my curiosity without requiring that I leave my house. That was another bond the dumb girl and I shared. We were both really lazy.

I did give that a try. When he finally phoned, I asked him, "What's the longest relationship you ever had?"

"Six years," he said.

"What happened?" I asked.

"Oh, you know," he said. "We grew in separate directions. We ended up wanting different things."

Platitudes, I thought. *The kind meant to leave me totally in the dark. Not a good sign. He doesn't want me to know what actually happened.*

Which of course is when he asked me out again. I had no reason not to say yes.

Because the physical contact had been so electrifying on the first date, I was worried about the second date, even as I pined for it. Things would escalate. Who was this guy I was hot for, anyway? What if I was headed for bed with another lunatic?

Research was going to be my salvation this time. I was not going to proceed blindly like before.

Of course, research had never been a specialty of mine so it was hard to know where to begin. Putting first things first, I decided I needed to find out who his last few girlfriends were and talk to them. I had to do this quickly. I had to have the data necessary to make an informed decision about him before the next hormonal explosion.

I started by asking around at my school to see if anyone knew any teachers who taught at Mike's school. Someone did. Keith McTeer, the other art teacher in my department, had a friend who taught French at that school. Begrudgingly he agreed to call him and ask about Mike.

"He says he used to date a woman named Nicole who taught third grade for a few years at that private girls' school in the Valley," Keith told me, "the West Valley School for Girls. He says he thinks she works at a temp agency now. And he was also married for a few years in the early nineties to a woman named Sharone. My source and his life mate went to dinner with them a couple of times. He thinks maybe she moved up to Ventura and is cutting hair at a salon."

Armed with this information, I immediately started doing nosier, pushier things than I have ever done before.

First I called up the West Valley School for Girls and asked to speak to the third-grade teacher named Nicole. They offered me the name of the agency she worked at with almost no prompting: AAAA Temps. It was walking distance from my house.

Next I went over there under the pretense that I was thinking about getting a part-time job. It was in a plain-looking office building, on the ground floor, between a pharmacy and a travel agency. I stood outside the door for quite a while, pretending to wait for someone, before I got up the courage to walk inside.

And there she was, sitting at a desk behind an engraved nameplate, packing up to leave for the afternoon. She was a slim, pretty, preoccupied-looking woman in her early thirties with longish light brown hair full of blond streaks. She was straightening up her desktop as she also put a lot of loose papers back into their designated files.

I would have gone up to her right then but I didn't want to seem like a stalker. Which is of course exactly how I felt and in a sense what I was.

I needed an angle that would make her trust me, make her comfortable enough to be willing to spill her guts to a stranger. I couldn't think of one so I pretended to be on some kind of generic fact-finding mission in search of a good temp agency. We smiled at each other, and I exited, too ill at ease to say anything but hello.

When I got home I called Ventura information. A jolt went through me when I realized that Mike's ex-wife was still using his last name. She was listed in the phone book!

Meanwhile my second date with Mike arrived. I didn't have the information I wanted about his past, but I couldn't have been more excited anyhow. Once again I detailed myself like a brand-new car. I whitened my teeth, I had my every body part waxed, followed by a facial, a steam, a seaweed wrap, a full-body scrub, and a massage. By the time I left that day spa I had been pounded, salted, rubbed with herbs and oils, then steamed and roasted over coals. I felt so much like a fancy hors d'oeuvre I half expected to see a toothpick decorated with cellophane sticking out of my head. And I was terrified, because I knew, where Mike was concerned, I was playing with fire.

The dumb girl, far from being dead, was alive and screaming out orders like a KGB officer. The smart girl shrugged her shoulders quietly, too sedated by pricey grooming procedures to have any active responses.

Once again, the date was more than a big success; it was a complete blast. We talked and talked. We went for a long walk on the beach, took off our shoes and walked in the surf, then made out, then talked some more. We went to a seafood restaurant overlooking an orange sunset and ate sushi. We looked like some kind of "falling in love" montage in a TV movie-of-the-week.

After that we went to see *Titanic,* a movie I had been carefully avoiding because watching people fall deeply in love right before they drowned in an icy sea didn't sound like my idea of a good time. But how wrong I was. Once we started to kiss, even as the assorted nautical nightmares played out on the screen, I got so overheated I came to think of *Titanic* as the feel-good hit of the season.

From that point on, my task was clear: to try and keep the dumb girl from talking me into going home with Mike or inviting him over to my place. There was no way that I could be in control with him in my home.

The dumb girl was really worked up. She wanted to leap on him like a lemming. So the smart girl kept moving our little date from one public gathering place to another.

"Have you ever been married?" I asked him as we sat down in the retro tiki lounge full of thirtysomethings who were pretending to be members of the Rat Pack and tried to pick something to drink out of a list of ridiculously creative cocktails. I was stalled, trying to decide between a martini marinara and a seaweed daiquiri. This seemed like a good time to try a little test to make sure he was leveling with me.

"Yes, for three years. In the early nineties," he said.

"What happened there?" I asked. "How come you guys came apart?"

"Well, she was kind of the rebound person, I think," he said. "I was really a mess. I had just come out of an eight-year thing that had really been a roller-coaster ride. The woman I was with before her was volatile. Crazy. Creative. Always changing her mind. At first I found it exciting but I got sick of how totally unstable she was. So when I met Sharone I liked that she seemed so placid. She was just kind of peaceful and quiet. I really liked that. Until I started living with it. Then it got really boring. She turned into a passive-aggressive person who didn't have anything on her mind except the ability to be unhappy about my every move and a general unwillingness to tell me what was wrong when I asked her."

A passive-aggressive person. That isn't any good, I thought.

"We never should have gotten married in the first place" is how he summed it up.

"What does she do for a living now?" I asked him.

"I heard she's cutting hair in Ventura," he said.

Yippee, I thought. He wasn't lying to me! Which made me love him so much that when he kissed me, the only reason I didn't wrestle him to the ground and start removing his clothes was because the tables were too close together and I would have ended up with my head in the lap of a woman in a short black dress. So I distracted myself by focusing on Dean Martin singing "That's Amore," visualizing the idea of someone getting hit in the eye by a bigga pizza pie. *Messy but not a serious injury un-less the cheese was very hot,* I thought.

Somehow I said good night to him. I got him to drive me back to where I had originally parked my car. Somehow I re-sisted the urge to pull him into my car with me. I don't know how I did it. Perhaps it was Divine intervention.

Once I got home I was so wired, I just sat in the bathtub and stared into space until every part of my body looked like an assemblage made of dried apricots. I relived each second of the entire evening, carefully making sure to add a paranoid nega-tive running commentary to every special moment so that I wouldn't get too carried away.

I was very proud that I managed to make it all the way through a second date without jumping into bed with him. But now the pressure was really on to learn what I needed to learn about his track record *fast.* I didn't know how long he would continue to play along with me pushing him off. Or how long I could control the increasingly irritable dumb girl. She was really horny and swearing at me like a drunken sailor on shore leave.

So the next day I decided to drive up to Ventura right after school. I would go in and out of hair salons until I found the ex-wife and I would just confront her.

How many hair salons could there be in Ventura? I thought to myself. *A lot more than I want to mess with* was the answer. My jaw dropped when I opened the phone book and saw that there were close to twenty. Who knew Ventura was such a hairstyling mecca? The dumb girl was out of patience, screaming at me to please give up and just forget the whole thing.

But I had come all the way here so I took a deep breath and started visiting the ones that were nearest by.

At the Hair Port, I asked if they knew where Sharone was cutting hair. They thought that maybe she worked at Hair Today, where it turned out she had worked for a couple of months a few years ago. Vance at Hair Today thought he had heard that she was at Hair Supply! But it turned out she wasn't. She had worked at Hair Supply! briefly, but had moved on to a better-paying position somewhere.

This brought me to the single weirdest act I have ever committed as an adult. I actually staked out her house. Not the same day—I went back the following morning really early, before the rush hour commute. I didn't have a first-period class. The timing was ideal. So I sat across the street in my car, pretending to read the paper, until I saw her come out the front door and get into her silver VW Beetle. She was a slim, tiny woman with longish light brown hair full of blond streaks. She was very pretty. Kind of a middle-aged version of Britney Spears.

Allowing her to get a safe distance ahead of me so she wouldn't notice that I was trailing her, I followed her a couple of miles to a place called the Hair Force. It is hard to explain how completely bizarre it felt living in a theatrical scenario that resembled something from a detective novel. It was enough to make me wonder if I was completely losing my mind. Which is why I was actually relieved when I checked my answering machine and realized I had forgotten about the meeting I had set up during first period with the principal to talk about funding for an after-school art program. I have always hated having to beg for funds. But now it sounded delightful. Begging for funds sounded warm and cozy compared to having to be a detective.

Despite discomfort and embarrassment at my methods, I

still felt the need to get the information I was after. And there was not much time left in which to do it. So during my lunch break, I called and made an appointment to have my hair cut with Sharone. She had an availability the following day, mid-morning. Which meant I would have to take a sick day off from work. Terrified though I was, I did it.

I arranged to have a fairly elaborate hair procedure in order to have enough time to bond with her and pull information out of her. I thought I would let her trim it but not style it. (After all, I didn't know if she was any good.) Then if I let her add a few streaks, that would take at least a couple of hours. Both of Mike's exes had streaks in their hair. Obviously he had a thing for girls with streaks. She knew how to do them. He would like them. Perfect.

I was a nervous wreck driving up there. I wasn't used to having such a mysterious and manipulative hidden agenda.

From the moment I walked past the big, terrible painting of the grinning cat in a rhinestone collar that hung on the wall in the waiting area of the salon, smelled that acrid, putrid smell of permanents in progress, and first laid eyes on Sharone, who was cleaning her workstation, I liked her a lot. She was easy to like, especially after I told her I had been hearing great things about her beautician skills from my friends. She was chatty and kind of smart. She had a sense of humor and an interesting sense of style. She was wearing leather wrist bands and a rhinestone dog collar around her neck, a black French-cut T-shirt that said DANGEROUS in rhinestones, and a pair of rolled-up jeans. She immediately started giving me compliments about the shape of my face. She knew a much better haircut for me than the one I was wearing. She thought the streaks were a great idea but she recommended red streaks instead of blond, and then making the rest of the hair blonder, then layering it for a fuller look. We would leave it longer in the front than in the back.

None of this sounded like anything I really wanted, although it did sound like a haircut my mother would have liked. But I felt so guilty about my creepy secret mission that I wanted Sharone to feel good about her work so she would like me.

After we had discussed my hair and our plans for my new cut, I waited a few minutes. Then, trying to seem as casual as possible, I started asking questions.

"I'm thinking about getting married in a couple of months," I began, "but I don't know how I feel about it. It seems like the percentage of marriages that succeed is so dismally low."

"Tell me about it," she said, lighting up a cigarette. "I was married for less than three years."

"Why do you think your marriage failed?" I asked her.

"Whew. Well, that's quite a can of worms," she said, exhaling dramatically. "Can you even get worms in a can? I wonder where that expression came from. They don't sell canned worms, do they? There are no airholes in cans. Wouldn't the canning part kill them?"

"I don't know," I said, trying to redirect her back to the original topic. My heart was beating so fast I felt faint. "If you want, I can look it up for you on the Internet. Why did you say you think your marriage failed?"

"I guess I didn't know him well enough before we got married," she said, after a long silence during which she sucked on her cigarette as she stared at a lock of my hair intently. "He kind of turned into a totally different guy than he was when I first met him."

"What did he seem like when you first met him?" I asked her.

"A lot of fun. He was sexy, we laughed a lot," she said. "He seemed really interested in me. He was easier to talk to than any guy I ever met."

I felt my veins filling with ice water.

"That sounds great," I said. "So what do you think went wrong?"

"Well, it was so perfect at first. . . . I guess that is why it hurt so much when it all changed. Men! Hmmph," she said, taking another drag of her cigarette and then putting it down on the edge of a full ashtray. "You know, I think the best way to go is a lot of thin little streaks instead of big ones because I think you might be missing an underlayer of your hair. Have you done a lot of bleaching before?"

"What exactly changed?" I asked her. I was upset enough by what I was hearing that I couldn't focus on an insignificant topic like my hair.

"Well, your hair is kind of brittle. Maybe you have a vitamin deficiency or something. But I think we could take care of it with a good conditioner," she said.

"No, no. I mean, with the guy you married," I repeated. How could I care about my hair, for Chrissake, when here she was spilling the beans?

"Well, after we got married his behavior was just different," she said. "The easygoing, fun guy was completely gone. Now everything had to be his way. And he would just completely ignore me when I talked. In fact, he couldn't put enough radios, TVs, and stereos on at the same time to drown me out. He bought a drum set and when I tried to discuss anything, he would start drumming! He got really mean about it, too. He would call me stupid."

"Wow, that's depressing," I said. "I went with a guy like that once."

"He was a lot like my dad, but I didn't see it till we got really close. That wasn't even the awful part. As soon as we got married, he totally lost interest in sex. He would just sit and watch TV, or talk on the phone. I couldn't prove it, because he paid the phone bill, but I think he was heavily into Internet porn by the time I finally left."

"Did you do anything to try to fix things?" I asked her.

"Well, I got him to go to therapy once," she said. "But he just sat there red-faced, furious. He wouldn't say a word, glaring at me until I felt like he had started to hate me. By the time it ended, I didn't know *what* was wrong or how to fix it. And he made me split the twenty-seven-hundred-dollar therapy bill. I thought that was cold."

"Wow, that sounds awful," I said to her. "I'm sorry that happened to you."

But what I was really thinking was that Mike's and Sharone's stories kind of matched up, in a *Rashomon* way. I was secretly thrilled that there was no way to determine where to place the blame.

Against my will and my own best interests, I was leaning toward her side of things. Right up until she combed out my hair.

I looked in the mirror and I saw the most hideous version of myself looking back at me. I was suddenly an emu. I couldn't recall ever having had a worse haircut. It was fluffy and flat, short and long, in all the wrong places. The bangs were too thin and too high on my forehead. The color was too Beverly-Hills-matron-trying-to-look-younger. It was rude. It was nasty. It would have been perfect for my birthday.

So nasty in fact that I stopped at the mall on my way home and bought a scarf, a hat, *and* a wig. I was ill prepared to look this awful in my everyday life. Maybe, I thought, the universe was getting back at me for messing around with the physics of my destiny.

Now I was doubly screwed. I was not just nervous about going out with Mike, I also looked too ugly to see him. Of course, the fact that this might destroy our chemistry should have been a *good* thing since I was trying to keep the sexual attraction in a holding pattern. Except that I didn't want to win by default. I wanted him to want me, even though I knew I really couldn't get involved. And I really couldn't get involved now that I had worked so hard to find out he had at least one terrible blot on his permanent record.

Even more appalling, I was too embarrassed to return to work. I knew I couldn't live through the expressions that would be on the faces of my students when they saw my incredibly gross new hair.

I really had no idea what to do. So I took Laurel and Janey out to dinner to test the waters. It was the first time I told anyone what I'd been up to.

The way they both widened their eyes, and then said nothing when I walked up to the table and they got a first look at my new haircut, provided more humiliation than I needed for the rest of the fiscal year. Things were off to a rocky start even before we got to the details of my bizarre new detective behavior.

"Well, I wouldn't cancel a date with a guy based on what his ex-wife said," said Janey. "No ex-wife thinks much of a guy who divorced her."

"Definitely go on the date with him," said Laurel. "But really keep your eyes open. And keep your scarf on."

"Tell me the truth. I look like Elton John, don't I?" I said, terrified that they would both say yes.

"The hair is *not* that bad," said Janey. "If you were a real estate saleswoman no one would say a thing. You could have your picture on a bus-stop bench with hair like that and be a big success."

"Len might ask you to wear a scarf over it if you worked at our store," said Laurel, who was by now working at the discount drugstore full-time. She was the purchasing agent in charge of seasonal gifts. "Not because it's so horrible or anything," she elaborated, "just because it's . . . you know . . . kind of alternative-looking for a place that sells Easter basket supplies and holiday Pez containers."

The reaction I got from my students was not that tactful. "She's trying to be more glamorous or something," I heard a tenth-grade girl say to her friend as they left for lunch. "My mother went through a phase like that. It has to do with worrying about getting old and not feeling very attractive."

"I think maybe she was wearing a wig yesterday," I heard the other one say. "Oh my God! I bet she has cancer!"

Which was just the ego bolstering I needed before a tension-filled social outing, but I went ahead and had our third date that very night. I wore a black, wide-brimmed felt hat that had hair sewn into it. Then I refused to remove it, period, until a strong gust of wind pushed it off and left me standing there grinning with embarrassment like an unmasked female impersonator.

After he finished reeling his eyeballs back into his head, Mike was totally and completely nice about the hair. At first he was concerned that I was ill. But after I assured him that I wasn't in chemotherapy, he was more puzzled than anything else.

"You looked great before," he said, "though I'm not saying there's anything wrong now. . . ."

"Oh go ahead, you can say it. I know it's grim," I butted in.

"No, no . . . it's not that bad. I just don't get why you decided to mess with the hair you had," he went on. "I guess that's a chick thing. My ex-wife was always screwing around with her hair. I'd leave for work with her looking great and come home to Larry from the Three Stooges."

It was impressive how there was still a crazy sexual tension building between us, despite the mess I'd made of myself. No matter what we talked about, we couldn't keep our hands off each other. He didn't understand why I was so reluctant to relocate to one of our homes where we could have what was obviously going to be some incredible fun. I barely understood myself. I was working off some very vague, very distant memory, theory, philosophy about the way I felt I should be conducting my life that was getting vaguer and vaguer as time went on. I was kind of a prisoner of too much information consumed from every angle on the topic of male/female relations, a great deal of which turned out to be self-canceling.

"I've been hurt a lot," I offered, "and I guess I want to make sure we are really going to have a relationship before I jump in with both feet and start producing those chemicals that women produce when they have an orgasm, which make us feel like we're more bonded than men who don't produce the chemicals at all."

"I understand, kind of," he said. "But I think we're going to have a great relationship. In fact, if I'm not mistaken, we're already having one."

After he said that, I really started having trouble remembering why we shouldn't have sex. He seemed reliable. When he said he was going to call, he did. We never ran out of things to say to each other. For someone I had only known a few weeks, I felt very good about him. If he were my employee, he'd have been in line for a handsome raise.

It took a lot of concentration and discipline for me to remember I hadn't completed the research I set out to do. I still needed to find out if his newly uncovered track record had a positive counterpoint or if his bad reviews were unanimous.

Somehow, through a combination of double-talk and real nervous vulnerability, I magically managed to put him off another week.

Meanwhile by now I was living in a state of such hyper-erotic fantasizing that it was nerve-racking trying to teach school. I worried that someone in one of my classes might have ESP and get a glimpse of the porno film starring me that kept starting up without permission in the screening room of my head.

I had bought myself one more date. But there was no way not to sleep with him this next time. If I pushed him away again, I was going to seem like someone who wasn't that interested or worse, beset with odd sexual issues. To say nothing of the fact that the dumb girl inside me was going to attempt a full-out coup if I kept ignoring her wishes. She was already threatening me with a full range of psychosomatic illnesses: backaches, neck aches, headaches, rashes, poor digestion.

So the next afternoon I went back over to the AAAA Temp

Agency to corner his old girlfriend Nicole. I sat through the chance to be interviewed by the agency director under the excuse that Nicole had come highly recommended. While I waited for her to finish interviewing an overweight, middle-aged man, I filled out forms that wanted to know about my job history, my educational background, and my psychological health. I briefly considered making every answer a lie. How I longed to write my occupation as a dental technician, and make my educational background a Ph.D. But I knew that, after a lifetime of never getting away with lies, somehow this would end up biting me in the butt. So I entered real answers.

"I used to be a teacher, too!" Nicole gushed at me as she reviewed my paperwork. "I still miss it! But after I got married and had a kid I needed to work fewer hours. You do know that we have no part-time jobs here that involve teaching?"

"Oh, I know, I know," I said.

"What kind of thing are you looking for?" she asked.

"What kind of thing do you have available?" I asked back.

"Well, for someone with your credentials, it's a pretty unimpressive list," she said. "About the best thing I can offer you is . . . oh my God, I feel terrible saying this, but it might not be that bad. . . . Have you done any receptionist work at all? Because they are looking for someone to work the reception desk at AAA Sick Room Supplies and Party Rentals?" She began dialing and before I could even respond, she had set up an appointment for me to meet the owners. With no idea what to do next, I tried to address the reason I had really come. But it was impossible. She was packing up her briefcase and running out to meet someone for lunch.

"You're meeting with Mr. Cooperman at four-fifteen," she

told me, handing me an appointment slip as she raced out the door. "He's hoping to hire someone today. Good luck!"

I was trapped. To ignore the appointment was to blow the connection to Nicole. So at four-fifteen I drove to Koreatown and sat in a row of folding chairs next to four other job applicants in the gray-on-gray room that was AAA Sick Room Supplies and Party Rentals. The window display said it all: crutches and wheelchairs, posed next to card tables laden with chafing dishes and champagne buckets. Every single moment that I continued to sit there was a moment I meant to run out the door. But I kept calming myself down, trying to focus on reading an article in a *People* magazine about celebrity marriages that had lasted less than three weeks.

Finally, Donald Cooperman, a short, heavy, mustachioed man, waddled toward me. He was wearing a pocket protector and the kind of orthopedic shoes that they mold to fit your feet.

"You are the woman sent by Nicole from AAAA Temp?" he asked, looking me up and down with a little too much intensity.

"Yes," I said. "But you can do so much better than me. I am really the wrong person for the job."

"Why do you say that?" he countered. "You look like a bright young woman. It says here you used to be a teacher?"

"Exactly," I said. "I know nothing about sales. I would be a thorn in your side."

"But you will maybe have the sensitivity to switch from the sickroom to the party, and then back again . . . yes? That is our challenge. One person wants the bedpans and hospital beds. That person is very depressed. Next person is throwing a birthday celebration and wants a piñata and a punch bowl. Totally different requirements, very challenging. You have to change moods all day long!"

"No, no," I said. "I know nothing about pleasing customers. You can do much better than me, I assure you."

"Why such a lovely girl like you has such bad self-esteem?" he countered. "I am sure you would do a wonderful job. You must learn to believe in yourself."

We went back and forth like this until I agreed to think it over. As with all my dealings with men, the more I said no, the more I resisted, the more he wanted me.

As soon as I could break away, I ran back to my car and headed back across town to try and talk to Nicole.

I arrived back at the temp agency just a few minutes before they closed.

"I had the strangest call from Mr. Cooperman," Nicole said to me. She was straightening up her desk, preparing to leave. "He wants to offer you the job but he's not sure you'll take it. What exactly is going on?"

It was then that I decided that creating an additional set of false pretenses under which to talk to her seemed spookier, more ghoulish, than just coming clean. I felt that honesty gave me more credibility, even with my hideous new hair. In fact, I was thinking that maybe the hair helped by making me appear more vulnerable and less threatening, albeit in a mentally disturbed sort of a way.

"I hope this doesn't sound too weird," I said to her, "but I was wondering if I could ask you a few questions about your old boyfriend Mike? I'm not really looking for a job. Can I talk you into having a cup of coffee with me for a couple of minutes?"

"Mike?" she said, shocked. "Where does this all come from suddenly? Are you with some law enforcement agency?" She was clearly alarmed. "Is he in some kind of trouble?"

"No, no . . ." I said. "I'm just someone who has started dating him."

Now she looked at me like I might be dangerous.

"Can I buy you a cup of coffee or something?" I asked her, knowing that she was going to refuse. Something about the way I was handling this was making her uncomfortable. I wondered if it was the bad karmic legacy of the ex-wife sending poison darts to the ex-girlfriend via my hideous haircut.

"What is this all about?" she asked, preferring to just sit quietly, at her desk, one hand on the phone in case she felt the need to call 911.

"I *know* this sounds loopy," I said to her. "Would it make you feel better if I told you I still teach art at Kennedy High? So how dangerous could I be? Although I guess I do have access to paint. I could probably stain your clothes pretty badly."

She not only didn't laugh, she continued staring at me suspiciously. The more I protested my sanity, the crazier it made me sound. I don't think it helped when I pulled out a bunch of IDs to show her—my school library card, my teacher ID, my driver's license—for no real reason at all.

"I met Mike a few weeks ago, and we've been dating. It's actually going really well," I said, chattering pointlessly like a stupid person on a really uncomfortable job interview, which is kind of what this was. "But I've been through so much pain with men in my romantic life that I'm completely gun-shy," I continued, hoping she was beginning to regard me as a little more benign. "It occurred to me that I really don't know anything much about him. So I decided to try and meet a few of his old girlfriends and find out what kind of damage trail he's been leaving."

"Wow. That's really weird," she said, "though it's actually kind of a great idea."

Praise the Lord, she was starting to relax with me.

"Why don't we go get that cup of coffee?" she suggested, pointing to the McDonald's that was right across the street. I have never felt more relieved.

And over cups of really old, acidy coffee, she said a lot of the same things I heard from Sharone the previous week.

"He started out just great," she said. "He was so much fun. Very attentive. Really willing to compromise. Interested in everything I said and did, interested in my family, my opinions, in making things right for me. But then as time went on he got more and more impatient, more and more dismissive. He never wanted to *do* anything except sit in front of the television and mope. He was pretty much tuning me out by the time he started sleeping days, staying up all night. He wasn't teaching that year. He was trying to be a writer. But he never sold anything. Possibly because he used to take his work and toss it in the fire every time he got frustrated. Those were the golden days when he punched holes in walls. I still have a knuckle print with his hair embedded in it in my den. A poignant and beautiful memento of our love.

"I think that's maybe when the cheating started," she went on. "I know that's when the sex stopped completely. Although, the whole thing ended so badly that it made me question whether or not he had ever been faithful."

"Do you think there's any reason to believe he's changed?" I asked her.

"Well, I knew someone who knew one of the girls he dated

after me," she said. "I was kind of following their thing for a while, out of my own morbid curiosity. He only lasted with her for a couple of months. I don't know what he's been up to since.

"I'm married now," she told me, as we were wrapping up, "so in a way, it was a blessing we broke up when we did or I never would have met the guy I married. But Mike taught me an important lesson about how the whole feeling of falling in love can be a really false read. What you think you feel about a person can change over time. It takes quite a while to be able to see it."

More horrible news. Unless I wanted to see it as *good* news. After all, I hadn't slept with him yet.

"I loved Mike so much," she continued, "I was willing to put up with anything for a while. But after Mike, I wound up with a guy who loved me more than I loved him. I was kind of noncommittal at first. Then one day, blammo, totally unexpectedly I fell in love back. And now it just gets better and better. Especially since the baby was born."

I thanked her for talking to me, then left depressed, deflated, confused. "This is smart, what you're doing, checking out his past," she said as we got into our cars to leave. "But I don't know what I am going to say to Donald Cooperman. He's going to be heartbroken when he hears you're not going to take that job. He thought you were a sickroom and party supply natural."

"Now what do I do?" I said to Janey. "What the hell do I do?"

"Well, you're supposed to cut the whole thing off at the knees," she said. "That was your motive for doing all the detective work. You got the answers you were looking for. He's a really bad risk. Now you have to face the truth and make some mature decisions that are in your own best interest."

"Yeah, but I haven't met anyone I've liked this well in years," I said. "How can I tell someone who is being so great to me to get lost? Does the past always determine the future? How do I know he hasn't really changed? Just because he was a shit to his last few girlfriends doesn't mean he's going to be a shit to me. That doesn't give him credit for being someone who might be interested in becoming a better person. He is so totally someone who would care about something like that. It also doesn't give *me* any points for being different than those women I just met. They were not like me! One was a terrible hairdresser and, okay, yes, the other one *used* to be a teacher. But she was a *grade* school teacher!! Which is very different than a high school teacher! Are we saying there is nothing at all unique about me that would have an effect on what might happen? I am telling you right now, those other women were nice. But they were not like me at all!"

"Well, then I guess you just did all that research for no reason," said Laurel.

I fretted over it all day and all night. Out of desperation, I even tried to talk it over with Dad, which of course was a huge mistake.

"You gotta be kidding me! You're going to evaluate a guy based on what his old girlfriends tell you?" Dad said. "Take it from me, that don't mean a damn thing. If you asked Evelyn or Anna Louise to talk about me, just imagine all the crazy crap they would tell you."

"Anna Louise?" I said. "You mean you two broke up?"

"Yeah, I knew she was playing me for a fool. Which I didn't mind. I was getting what I wanted. The sex was hot. Right up until the time where she thought she could weasel me into supporting her. She wanted to quit that cushy job she had at the Psychic Hotline. I said, 'No way am I ready for this kind of bullshit again.' Some psychic she turned out to be, huh?"

He broke out laughing so hard, it made me start to laugh, too.

"She obviously couldn't read me. I turned out not to be as stupid as she thought," he said.

"Wow, she was a telephone psychic? I didn't know she was a psychic," I said, immediately beginning to worry that she had been one of the people I consulted on the phone during my psychic binge. "I thought you seemed to be enjoying each other."

"She was enjoying every three-dollars-and-ninety-nine-cent minute she spent around me, as long as I had my wallet out. You don't notice a thing like that because you walk around with your eyes closed all day long. Your mother did it for forty-two years. The two of you. A sleepwalking society. Yeah, she was a psychic. Some psychic. She didn't see this one coming from a mile away. If this Mike seems like a good guy, listen to your dear old Dad who is trying to tell you to reel him in. You hear what I'm saying? I'm your father and I'm telling you that you're not getting any younger. What kind of a choice does a woman your age really have these days? If you've got a guy who seems interested in you, grab him before he gets away."

"Thank you, Dad, for totally destroying what was left of my generally shaky self-image," I said to him. "Thank you for reminding me that you see me as desperate and needy."

"What are you talking about?" he said. "You're just like your mother. So sensitive about every little thing. You can't stand it when I interject a note of reality to the conversation."

"Dad," I said, "is there anything I could say or do to make you stop hurting my feelings all the time?"

"What do you mean hurting your feelings?" he said, genuinely confused. "How am I hurting your feelings? You're my daughter. To me, you always look as beautiful as you did when you were sixteen. Better even. You had too much weight on you when you were a teenager. Which I told you repeatedly but you wouldn't listen then either."

"See? You just did it again," I said. "Why did you have to mention my weight as a teenager?"

"You're too sensitive," he said. "You know as well as I do that you were a kind of a porky kid."

"Dad," I said, "this is something I've really been wanting to talk to you about. You know how Mom and I always fought when she was alive? Now she's gone. We went through our entire mother/daughter cycle never able to make things any better."

"You two just never got along," he said. "You were always jumping down her throat."

"I don't want to start arguing the point again that she started most of the fights," I said to him. "I know you think she didn't. You don't have to believe me. But I'd like to find a way to get along better with you."

"Fine. Maybe you would prefer if we just stop talking altogether?" he said, starting to pout.

"No," I said, "that's where I left off with Mom. What I would really prefer is for you to try pausing to consider whether what you are going to say is going to make me 'sensitive' and if you think the answer is yes, maybe just don't say it. Like, for instance, you don't have to point out to me that you don't like how I look. Or that you think I'm getting older. I know I'm getting older. I'm not always pointing out to you that you're getting older."

"Well, that's because that stuff doesn't really matter when you're a man," he said.

"I just want you to understand that it does me no good to hear about how inadequate you think I am," I said.

"I never said you were inadequate. Obviously I think you're adequate. You're my daughter. Adequate genes run in the family! But are you telling me you don't want a little fatherly constructive feedback?" he asked earnestly.

"No. I really don't," I said. "I've had enough for one life-time. I hear your voice in my head, criticizing me, even in my sleep. I still hear Mom's voice, telling me that I'm too fat and too thin, that my hair is too short and too long. And she isn't even on the planet anymore."

He shrugged. "Whew. You got bigger problems than I thought."

Then he paused. "That wasn't a criticism. Plenty of people have bigger problems than I thought." He paused again and looked at me nervously, to see if I was going to explode at him. I said nothing.

"So I guess from what you're saying, you think maybe I overdid it a little. Geezo peezo. Nobody ever wants to hear the truth. You know what they call that? It's called kicking the mes-senger." Then he sat there quietly, looking deflated.

I wanted to apologize but instead I sat there quietly, too.

"What the hey," he finally said, shrugging his shoulders. "Sure. Why not?"

It was maybe the single nicest thing he ever said to me.

"I would really appreciate it," I said. "I'd love for us to try and be closer if we could."

"I got no problem with that," he said. And then we hugged. My eyes filled up with tears.

The next few weeks I noticed him trying to hold his tongue around me. Watching him making an effort, no matter how minimal, was very touching. Even a moment's hesitation when it was clear he wanted to attack me struck me as very moving. It was nice to think that maybe before he checked out we could actually develop some kind of a real friendship. Of course, every time I got too hopeful he jumped me and sucker-punched me with something weird.

Like when he suggested that I give my phone number to a restaurant maître d' who was doting over us, pretending to like us, offering us false friendship and more coffee. Not only was he at least sixty and strange-looking in a cobra-esque kind of way, he was clearly gay.

"How do you know he's gay?" my father said. "You can't go around prejudging everyone like that."

"Because I just know he's gay," I said to him. "He's obviously gay."

"Don't be such a know-it-all," he replied. "You always find a crazy reason to ignore my advice. I've been on this planet a few more years than you have and I am here to tell you that when a guy is really acting gay, that usually means he *isn't* gay. When they're really gay, they hide it."

At that point, the date with Mike was looming. I was really looking forward to it. I knew I wasn't going to just throw him away because of what he had done to an ex-wife and an old girlfriend. After all, I said to myself, if I learned anything from my exhaustive research into quantum physics, it was that the Heisenberg uncertainty principle tells us that nothing can be predicted with real certainty. Like a photon, Mike's behavior was essentially and inescapably unpredictable. The best I could ever know were the probabilities, to say nothing of the fact that the very act of trying to measure his behavior affected and changed the result.

For all I knew the two other women had been the ones who had driven *him* nuts. Maybe they both had bad combinations of traits that brought out his worst qualities. Maybe they had taught him important lessons that had caused him to change. Maybe I had the magic key that would unlock his best self.

That next date we had sex. It was incredibly great. It was like a big, hot, wet, flaming ice-cream sundae. It was sweaty. It was chilling. It was tender. It seemed personal and raunchy and endearing and athletic and comfortable. It was everything I ever wanted in a sexual experience, including a real orgasm and a call from him as soon as he got home. To top it all off, I finally achieved a goal I never thought would be mine: I became the newest member of the And-Michaels. And not a moment too soon since a position had just opened after James and Michael unexpectedly called it quits.

So here it is my birthday again, and I have been seeing him for almost four months, during which I have been happy and at the same time a nervous wreck in as many of the eleven dimensions I know how to occupy.

A book I read said not to judge a relationship until after the three-month mark because until then everyone is still on their best behavior. We just hit the three-month mark a couple of weeks ago. I am actually afraid to say anything more for fear of jinxing something. I don't want the dumb girl to start lecturing me because she wants more attention, wants to obsess, feels needy, and wants commitments. I would like this to be the year when the dumb girl relocates to one of the eleven dimensions that cannot be reached for the rest of her life. She has never given me anything but terrible advice. I wish I could convince her to go study with the Dalai Lama and not come back until she has changed her views of everything.

Which brings me to the flowers again. This year I didn't have nearly the emotional reaction to them as in previous years. I was distracted by my continuous emotional reaction to Mike. So I decided that if Carl was going to continue sending them, I would simply continue thanking him. There was no other piece of behavior that made any sense. If the white flowers meant truce, then so be it. A truce was okay with me.

I sat down to write him a thank-you note regarding his thoughtful gift. No special paper purchase. No special wacky lettering or funny drawings. Just a small rectangular Hallmark card that said "thank you" in script on the front. As I was writing it, I felt so calm and detached that I began to remember all the good stuff we had together. Like how we would make popcorn and watch TV. Okay, so it was hardly ever the shows I liked. And I had to make the popcorn, and then get up in the middle of the show to make some more, not to mention special separate trips for napkins and more salt and to melt some more butter. But I didn't care. At least we were doing something together. If you could call eating popcorn and watching TV "doing something together."

Then there was the way we always ate breakfast together. Okay, yes, I had to *cook* the breakfast. Not everyone can be a monument to breakfast preparation like Dad. But I didn't mind.

Sometimes we went out to breakfast at this one place I really loved that had weird, poorly rendered paintings on the walls of jazz musicians whose arms were too short for their torsos. I used to like the place because they added a lot of unusual things to eggs, like caviar or lima beans or chocolate chips (a bad idea though I gave them points for originality). That used to be a lot of fun. Even though Carl would mainly just disappear behind the sports section or the business section and barely say a word to me. But it was the companionship I liked. It was better than being alone.

Or was it? It occurred to me that I had never had the nerve to go there alone.

So yesterday I went to Dizzy's all by myself and ordered the chocolate chip omelette. It was still pretty horrible. Yet I was surprised to see that even alone, it was a fair amount of fun. (Though now I was the one who disappeared behind a large section of newspaper. It was the only way I could think of not to seem too pathetic eating alone in a big room full of cute couples and medium-sized family gatherings. There is no more intense reading than the kind you have to do when you want other people not to think it is sad that you are dining alone.)

I found myself wondering if it was Carl that I missed or the things we used to do together that I was too chicken to do alone. Once I manage to figure that out, maybe I will be able to stop feeling weird and paranoid about the fact that I already can't seem to get Mike to go anywhere with me.

What I Learned This Year:

1. No more trying to spend my birthday alone. But if there's something to do besides spend it with Dad, do that. Otherwise, seek out friends. *Any* friends. Even secondary or tertiary friends. Make some new friends if necessary.

2. Remember not to tell Dad anything personal. And if I do, remember not to be too sensitive about how he responds. He at least seems to be trying now. I have to do the same.

3. Have the courage to make weird new clothing purchases on my own but do *not* extend this kind of courage to weird new hair. If I ever get my old hair back, remember to leave it alone.

4. No more running around doing a clandestine search on someone before I go out with him. Trust my instincts if it seems to be going okay. Because I apparently am not going to pay attention to the research that turns up anyhow.

5. Just write Carl polite thank-you notes. Don't take it personally if I don't hear from him.

6. Analyze what I miss about Carl. Then go do the same shit by myself. And see if I really miss Carl. Or if I just miss myself.

7. Don't expect anything from Mike. Take it one day at a time.

What I Learned About Science This Year:

In quantum physics I read that the act of measuring a particle changes it. Which makes me think I may have wrecked everything and caused everything to change with Mike by the act of trying to measure him.

Fortymmmmppphhh

TODAY I AM LOOKING PAST the barrel of the most exhausting birthday yet.

Started out the day with a bang by going to an appointment with a psychic/masseuse/nutritionist that Laurel and Janey bought me for a present. They both swear by him, even though he made Janey bring all her leather goods into his office so he could cleanse and detoxify them.

"I think the leather item he really wants is your wallet" is what I told her.

"No no," she said. "You gotta try him. He can rub your neck, tell you about the past life that is blocking your energy, and align your spine at the same time."

He had me lie down on a gurney and moved my arms and legs around for a few minutes. Then he pronounced me depressed because of my pathetic, disconnected love life. I found this extremely unnerving because until he said it I was under the impression that I was in a pretty good mood. Then I started to worry that even my good moods could be classified as depression.

He told me that my brain's neurological pathways, the very pathways whose function was required for a successful relationship, were "in exile." And that I would never have any success in love until he helped me reroute them. I guess he was going to lead them back to the cheery little neurological community center where everyone else's better-adjusted pathways were hanging out.

Toward this end, he ran a laser beam over me and put drops of something on my collarbone. When I reached over to read what was in the drop bottle, all it said was FEAR: HIBISCUS, TIGER LILIES, AND JUNIPER BERRIES. He informed me that many such treatments would be necessary if I was to ever get my brain pathways out of pathway prison at a cost to me of about $150 a pop. I wondered if I negotiated with the good doctor, whether I could get a few of them at a time out on probation for a lower rate.

After that, my exiled pathways and I went out to dinner with Dad. Okay, I know I said last year no more birthday dinners with Dad if there was any kind of reasonable alternative. But there wasn't. Mike was out of the question. I'll get to that in a minute. And Janey and Laurel both were otherwise occupied.

Janey got a job looking for people to go on nightmarish dates for a new TV show. She asked me to please come try out. I said no because it conflicted with teaching. Considering the amount of nightmarish dates I've dealt with these past few years, I no longer find them of even marginal entertainment value.

Laurel was having marital difficulties. "I'm starting to think Len is a big dolt," she said. "The most interesting thing about him is the discount he gets us on holiday decorations." She's apparently developed a big crush on some blow-dried soap opera actor who shops in the pharmacy of Len's store. "We had a big huge discussion on throat lozenges the other day," she said, glowing. "He'd never tried any of the herbal ones and he was really interested in my take on them. I mean, there he was, all sick and congested. And we were discussing lozenges . . . and I was thinking to myself how much more interesting and attractive and just plain fun he was than Len."

About a week later she called to ask me if I had noticed that Len was an asshole. She was seriously thinking about leaving. A couple of days after that she phoned again to say that she was trying to get pregnant because, whether or not she stayed with Len, she felt he would make an excellent father.

So my birthday was a family affair again, in a manner of speaking. This year Dad brought his newest girlfriend, Lynetta, a retired grade school teacher from Louisiana. She immediately struck me as perfect for him, having spent a lifetime perfecting the art of being patient with uncomprehending children. I knew he was home free when she smiled and said nothing while he told her how to eat soup. I have yet to really determine whether or not she even listens when he talks. If she doesn't it could be for the best.

The only negative is that they may be too much alike as she also explains extremely simple procedures in mind-boggling detail. "What kind of sauce is this?" opened up a forty-minute discussion on the little-known differences between a sauce and a gravy. (She claimed backing from *Webster's Dictionary* when she insisted that a sauce was stewed fruit whereas a gravy is made of the juice that drips from meat. Ah . . . but that was only her opening volley.)

We all went to dinner at a Chinese restaurant that Dad and Lynetta both liked. It had a line of people waiting for tables ahead of us. This, of course, provoked a huge fight between the maître d' and Dad because we had made a reservation. Or so Dad insisted. The maître d', who after all was in a position to know these things, claimed that they never take reservations. They had had a first-come, first-served policy, period, ever since the place opened eight years ago. Fortunately the maître d' spoke almost no English. I was glad he could only understand a mere portion of what was being said because my father was behaving so rudely you would think it was the culmination of a lifelong grudge. His beet-red face and loud voice got the attention of everyone in the restaurant as well as giving the uncomprehending maître d' a pretty good idea of what the words he didn't understand might mean.

I, of course, stood quietly by and watched another dining population begin to regard us with contempt. But this year I had a new perspective to add to the mix. I made a conscious choice to take comfort in the idea that this was a distinct and unusual birthday tradition original to my family.

"A birthday really isn't a birthday to us without a nice big screaming fight in a restaurant," I said to myself. "Therefore I welcome it, and embrace it as part of my special heritage. As with the changing of the seasons, a screaming restaurant fight both connotes the passage of time and celebrates the fact that I was born."

I was able to do this because after months of Janey begging me to go to classes with her, I'd been going to yoga. I resisted at first: I had no interest even after she trotted out the fact that she sometimes saw David Duchovny and Heather Graham in class.

Then one day after a big fight with Mike I said yes and to my great surprise got hooked on the combination of spiritual positivism and excellent bicep development. I liked the "push yourself to the edge and then release it" idea. I also liked the fact that at long last I had something in common with Madonna.

But back to the big birthday: We finally were seated at a table that my father pronounced not clean enough, not large enough, and too near the front entrance. I tried to embrace that as a sign that things were going predictably well.

"Thank you, God," I said quietly, "for remembering to include every familiar detail again in these my annual birthday festivities." In yoga we learn to try to do everything possible in a pose, or asana as we call it, and then to release it.

The best news of all was that my father was really hungry and raring to order. Not so hungry that he didn't first call the management over to argue about whether the crab in the crab and shrimp lo mein was really crab or, as he suspected, a crab substitute like pollack. I remembered to thank God and the Universe that he was hungry enough to want to start eating as soon as his food came, temporarily slowing down his ability to argue. A full stomach always took a little of the edge off his vitriol. I felt gratitude and then I released it.

This lapse in the action gave Lynetta an opening to ask what had happened to that nice young man I was seeing. My father, despite a mouth full of lo mein, grunted *no* at her, then gave her a look that stopped her dead in her tracks.

"Lynetta, for crying out loud. . . . What the hell are you trying to do to me? Don't start in with her on her birthday! She'll accuse us of intentionally hurting her feelings!" he said before I even found the need to make cryptic remarks about the condition of my brain pathways. That he thought to say this on my behalf was the best birthday present he could have given me.

Which brought us to the main event—the annual toast and gift-giving torture that is my payoff for growing a year older. It seemed like kind of a good omen when Dad offered his least-offensive toast ever.

"I'm not saying a damn thing! I'm afraid to say *anything* around you anymore because I know you'll get all bent out of shape if I even *mention* your age. God only knows what else I'm not supposed to say so . . . Happy Birthday, honey." In its way, it was very beautiful.

Then out came the gift box. I opened it slowly, taking time to try and intuit who made the purchase.

It was an odd, boxy-shaped pink cardigan sweater edged with a decorated ribbon full of beads shaped like little flowerlets, and it had a large orange-and-black cat decal stitched on the back. It came with a matching scarf. Clearly it had been selected by Lynetta. And it was just as inappropriate as anything I had ever been given by my own mother. This also warmed my heart, because it made me think that, if she could stick it out, Dad had truly found another suitable life partner.

"It's beautiful," I lied.

"Honey, it will look fantastic on you. Go try it on," said Lynetta.

"No, I never try things on in restaurants. But thank you just the same," I said, rewrapping the box. Which, to my recollection, is the exact moment that the second fight began. It started when my father turned and glared at the guy at the next table who was talking very loudly into his cell phone.

"Bud," the cell phone guy was saying, in too high a volume to be ignored, "I had to cancel our two o'clock for next Thursday. I think it is premature for us to meet until the full set of contracts are signed." He was completely surprised when my father tapped him on the shoulder.

"Hey pal," my father said to him, "how about bringing the volume down? Tell Bud you'll call him back after dinner."

"Get your hand off me," said the cell-phoner. "I'm not your pal. And I don't see where this is any of your business."

"You made it my business because you're sitting an inch from my ear screaming into the goddamn phone like you're yelling to someone across the street. I came here to celebrate my daughter's birthday, not to listen to your goddamn fucking phone calls," said my father.

"I'd punch you right in your ugly face, you shriveled-up old fart," said cell phone guy, "but you'd probably have a heart attack, not die, and then sue me." Which took us precisely to the moment when the restaurant deployed a group of waiters to our table carrying a small cake to sing a pidgin English, barely comprehensible version of "Happy Birthday."

Remembering to be yogic, I did what I could to embrace the joy and the light in listening to underpaid, newly immigrated employees from backward countries in the throes of frightening political turmoil pretending to celebrate the birthday of someone they have never laid eyes on while all around us a restaurant full of people filled with loathing sent hate vibes toward our table.

So I filled my heart with gratitude that I did not have any

one of a number of life-threatening illnesses. Then, to keep myself distracted, I quietly named them all: tuberculosis, muscular dystrophy, ulcerative colitis, amyotrophic lateral sclerosis, rickets, scleroderma, alopecia, diverticulitis, malaria, cancer (breast, brain, lung, ovarian, skin, cervical, uterine, stomach, bone), retinitis pigmentosa, bubonic plague, glaucoma, schizophrenia, polio, vertigo, elephantiasis, degenerative arthritis, lupus, pink eye, Alzheimer's, Parkinson's, tinnitus, leprosy, thrush, cystic fibrosis, Raynaud's phenomenon, pyorrhea, myocardial infarction, nephritis, meningitis, irritable bowel syndrome, gallstones, cluster headaches, anemia, cerebral palsy, chlamydia, panic disorder, Hantavirus, endometriosis, leukemia, tardive dyskinesia, spastic colon, acid reflux, mad cow disease, manic depression, clinical depression, diabetes, multiple sclerosis, syphilis, HIV, hypoglycemia, vaginal warts, cancer (throat, bladder, lymph, pancreas), Crohn's disease, Tourette's, that lung disease where you need an oxygen tank, ileitis, arteriosclerosis, macular degeneration, a really bad bladder infection, osteoporosis, agoraphobia, meningitis, hepatitis, stomach flu, pancreatitis, plantar's warts, typhoid, herpes, cirrhosis, trichomonas, strep throat, Munchausen by proxy, Graves' disease, bleeding ulcers, scurvy, scarlet fever, smallpox, gangrene, toxic shock syndrome, that flesh-eating virus, rabies. Happy Birthday to me.

When we got up to leave, I thought I heard a small round of applause coming from the kitchen. I decided to think of this as my birthday card from the Universe even though it was probably an expression of relief on behalf of the restaurant staff that we were finally vacating all the obvious dimensions of the premises.

But of course, there was more fun still to be had.

When Dad and Lynetta dropped me off at my house, after a car ride full of repeated rage-filled recountings of the cell phone fight, resupplied with new endings and other versions of the things my father *should* have said and done to that god-damn bastard, there sitting out on the front steps of my house were of course the fucking flowers. This year the most perfect bouquet of three dozen pink- and peach-colored roses I had ever seen. They were arranged in a ball, their stems all trimmed so that they came together like a big head of curly rose blossom hair.

I took them into the house alone and sat there staring at them. The card was the same. Happy Birthday Carl. But this year they made me sentimental again, probably because the breakup with Mike had just happened.

I was trying to figure out what had gone wrong and I guess I was still too emotional and confused because I found it all caroming into the same set of issues that caused me to break up with Carl.

It all started during month four when it seemed to me that Mike was getting short with me. He had started to snipe and act critical. He suddenly didn't really like the way I dressed, no matter what I wore. One day he wanted me to dress sexier, more feminine, but then when I put on a tight skirt and high heels, he complained that I didn't walk fast enough.

"There's a reason no one wears four-inch heels in track events," I said to no one since he was a block ahead of me.

I was especially unnerved by the way he would stare off when I asked him questions. I noticed he would pick up a magazine and page through it while I was trying to talk to him.

In a way, he was beginning to seem so much like my mother that I almost bought him a Mother's Day card. How could I have done it again? Found my mother *again*?

On top of that, it seemed to me we were running out of things to say to each other right about the same time he started to go out for a lot of drives all alone. I thought about following him, but I had a new rule: no more detective work. I was too exhausted and too newly yogic to continue playing detective.

I tried to be very careful about not acting like I was feeling bored, as kind of a counterpoint to his restless behavior. So I would sit for hours, staring in the direction of the television, pretending to be following a football game or a hockey game he wanted to watch, trying to think of it as a form of meditation, or secretly using the time to create new lesson plans in my head. (In fact, it was during the football play-offs that I came up with one of this year's best assignments: Do a drawing of someone watching television, and then in the TV monitor make a drawing or collage that shows how the person in front of the set is really feeling about their life.)

I really didn't know what had gone wrong with Mike.

I tried amping up the sexual connection by renting X-rated videos, which I think he kind of liked—even though he would make me go up to the cashier to rent them. He was too embarrassed to stand there while the slacker dudes at the register yelled out, "*Nasty Nurses.* Due back five o'clock Wednesday."

During this phase of things, I went with him to a strip club. It sounded sexy until I actually stepped inside. Sitting there, feeling overdressed, my purse hugged to my chest, wearing glasses and worrying about the emotional well-being of the dancers, while at the same time wondering if Mike was sorry he wasn't dating a stripper, made me feel like a member of some brand-new, unidentified third sex. I felt like Margaret Mead at her senior prom. Janet Reno in a fluffy pink party dress. I have never felt more like I was in the wrong place at the wrong time than I did that night.

I took codependency to a whole new level by being unable to stop empathizing with this one stripper, Toffee, who I didn't think could dance.

"Guys don't come here expecting 'Ode to Terpsichore,'" Mike said to me, rolling his eyes. But I was humiliated on her behalf, imagining myself up there on the runway, unable, like her, to figure out an effective way to work the aluminum pole into my choreography. I felt like I could hear her worrying: "Oh boy, I bet I should have applied some self-tan before I left the house! I wonder if I run out right now I could still find a tanning parlor that's open. It would be more than worth it to brave skin cancer in exchange for the peace of mind that comes from knowing that my butt doesn't have uneven orange streaks. Dear God, whose idea was this damn aluminum pole anyway? Someone, quick, get me the classified section of the *Times*!"

That night I started faking orgasms again. I did it so he wouldn't think that I thought sex with him was a part of our problem. I also didn't want him to think that any of my short-comings were getting in the way. Or that I was trying to make him over into something he wasn't. I was trying to keep my own record really clean.

I think this is when I started getting those lectures from him about how men need variety. About how it isn't really natural for a man to be tied down to just one woman. About how women want to make men into something that nature never intended them to be. Men need to spread their seed. Men need variety, men need polygamy, men need blabbitybla. Blablabla.

The first time I heard the speech I was hurt and paranoid. The next time I was hurt, paranoid, and pissed. The third time I couldn't keep myself from screaming out, at full volume, "Who gives a fuck what nature intended? We are a long, long way from natural living, mister. Nature didn't intend for us to use money or forks or washing machines or cell phones or CD players. Nowhere in nature is there gum surgery or porno films or microwaves or pizza or sweatpants or cars or computers. Nothing we do, nothing at all, has anything to do with nature. So why don't you and all the other so-called nature boys who are so keen on living by nature's laws go find yourselves a nice underground cave to hang out in. That way you could have this conversation over and over again with someone who cares!"

We broke up after that. Then we got back together when he insisted he didn't mean it and he really wanted me and only me. I was the one. That lasted a couple of weeks and then the nature lectures resumed. So we broke up again only to get back together three weeks later for two more weeks. The next time I had a lecture about natural men, I changed my phone number. Nature didn't intend for us to have just one phone number, I told him.

Of course, this was the year where I saw my own reflection looking really nasty in the form of Monica Lewinsky. It seemed to me she was dying for the sins of dumb and crazy girls of all ages everywhere. Never before had I seen the paradigm of crazy dumb girl syndrome so publicly X-rayed, examined, dissected, and analyzed. I saw myself in her in a million different ways that were painful and embarrassing to acknowledge.

Starting with how she obsessed endlessly about the details of each encounter with her boyfriend the president as though he was a dude she met at a dance club who was speaking to her in secret code.

When I read her quote, "The first time I looked in his eyes I saw something that I didn't expect to see," I immediately thought about how many times I had noticed that something in someone's eyes and been confused by it. It reminded me of the millions of times the dumb girl tried to convince me that every moment of chemistry with a new guy was a crescendo in a symphonic love overture. I think it took me until this year to finally realize that when you see too much in his eyes in the very beginning, you're not looking at the early stages of love, you're looking at the early stages of trouble.

So I guess I just learned again that embarking on the greatest love the world has ever known with someone you barely even know is like boarding a sinking cruise ship, no matter how many simultaneous all-you-can-eat buffets are part of your pre-paid package.

Watching everything unravel with Mike made me feel like the dumb girl had never really relinquished the controls. Like I never learned a damn thing. It made me wonder if I was even an important element in the whole romance, or if it would have happened just that way with whoever would have run into him while he was perusing Martin Amis's books at the bookstore that night.

So *this* has to be the year where I will definitely stop dating versions of my parents. I thought I fixed that last year and the year before and the year before that. But now I see I never fixed it at all. No more kidding around. I've got to knock it off.

I think the thing that really held me back from fixing it before was the fear that if I didn't jump toward all the people who attracted me I would look around one morning and notice that now I was way, way into the Hole and maybe even headed for the board of directors. I was suddenly an esteemed Hole veteran.

I don't believe I am in the Hole. I think that maybe I was Hole eligible after things came apart with Mike. Maybe I was tottering dangerously on the precipice. But I got my balance and instead of stumbling in I set up housekeeping in a little gully that was Hole adjacent. And that's where I'm planning to hang out for as much time as it takes for me to reorganize my molecules so I won't keep getting involved romantically with versions of my parents.

It feels wrong to say that I really *like* spending time alone. It definitely took some getting used to. It started out humiliating, trying to cope with an obstacle course of a million different socially unsettling predicaments. I couldn't bear being seen eating dinner by myself in a restaurant. I was always the only person all alone. On rare occasions, I would see another solo person and feel a sense of relief . . . whew, it isn't just me after all. Then ten minutes later the other person's dinner date would arrive.

So I spent a ridiculous amount of time trying to figure out what expressions to wear on my face to counteract my discomfort. I would open with something that looked like I was so distracted by my constantly busy life that I was lucky to have a few minutes to myself. Then I would follow up with trying to convey a sense that I was meeting some incredibly cool people later. This was sometimes so much work it was difficult to chew my food. Which is why for a while I tried to work on the premise that I was invisible. This was hard to maintain when a waiter would come to take my order.

After that I tried out a "Fuck everyone. I am here by myself and I'M PERFECTLY HAPPY!" face. But all that hostility was incompatible with digestion.

Finally I began to either bring along a book or get my food to go.

Learning to attend parties alone was the final frontier. I used to attach myself like a barnacle to the first person willing to talk. That came with a different set of problems because the people most willing to collect barnacles were inevitably the biggest shipwrecks in the harbor.

Now I try to imagine myself as a skulking woman of mystery. I enter alone. I leave alone in a puff of smoke. I disappear like a jaguar into the jungle at night. Like a cougar, a puma, or a lynx, whichever one of those large cats has the most exiled brain pathways.

Anyway, this year when I finally got home from my happiest of birthdays, I sat down with a pad of paper and began to make a list of the good and bad in my relationship with Carl. I was feeling melancholy. The goddamn flowers pushed me over the edge.

The "Good" list included silly little endearing stuff like dancing and singing and making jokes after too many beers. The "Bad" list included the time he accused me of fucking around on him when I was an hour late coming home from shopping. And how he would scream at me and call me a castrating cunt when I would do or say things I never imagined would upset him. Sometimes "Feel like going to a movie?" was all it would take to push him over the edge.

Then his face would freeze into an ice-cold expression. The more I thought about it, the more he sounded exactly like Dad.

The "Bad" list really outweighed the "Good" by about five

to one. But "Good" still brought up powerful memories that made me want to know why in God's name he was still sending me flowers. Was there something between us that could still be salvaged? Were the flowers a pack of seeds I was supposed to plant?

This would be the year when I would get to the bottom of the flower puzzle.

So I drank two wineglasses full of hot sake. And I called him.

And when he didn't answer, I called him at work.

And when the assistant said he wasn't in, I didn't give up. I found out when he would be in and called him back.

Finally I cornered him.

"Hi," he said, not indicating any particular emotion he might be having at hearing the sound of my voice after all this time.

"Hi," I said.

There was a long pause.

"I guess you're wondering why I am calling you, huh?" I finally said.

"Well, we exchanged calls a while back," he said. "So . . . uh . . . nice to hear from you. How is everything? How are your folks? Everything good?"

"One is in love. The other one is dead. But that's not why I'm calling," I said. "I'm calling to thank you in person for the beautiful flowers. They are really lovely. This year might be the loveliest bunch yet."

At first he said nothing. Then, "Oh. Good. Good. I'm glad you like them."

When he lapsed back into silence, his silence spurred me on.

"Do you mind me asking why exactly you send them?" I said. "I mean, we broke up seven years ago. That's kind of unusual to be sending flowers to an old girlfriend for seven years after the breakup, don't you think?"

He continued saying nothing. But it was much too late for me to retreat now.

"I was wondering what it all meant. I thought maybe you wanted me to call or something. But now that I have you on the phone, it doesn't seem like that is how you are acting. Or is it? Did you mean for me to call you?"

He sighed.

"Well," he said, sighing a second time. "I think there's some misunderstanding."

After a rather lengthy pause, he started again.

"So what you are saying is that you are getting flowers from me on a regular basis?"

If I were a cartoon, my eyes would have started rotating in opposite directions as birds making cuckoo clock sounds began circling above my head.

"Just on my birthday," I said, "which was yesterday."

"Oh, that's right! Happy birthday!" he said. "So I sent you flowers on your birthday! Great! That's great! What kind?"

"This year a couple dozen pink- and peach-colored roses," I said, "which the florist's dictionary says mean 'perfect happiness' and 'desire,' in case you're interested."

"Gee . . . well, terrific!" he said, and then paused. "I think I know what's happened. You are on Sela's Rolodex. I guess she never crossed you off when we broke up. Fucking Sela. No wonder I'm always broke."

Now I sighed. And then I broke out laughing so hard I was blowing bubbles out of my nose. It was pure hysteria.

"So you never even knew they were coming?" I said, composing myself.

"Well, no, not really. But I'm not mad that she sent them or anything. I mean I'm happy you got some nice flowers on your birthday. You deserve them. A real *big* arrangement, were they?"

"Yep," I said, realizing he was now worrying about the price tag. I could hear him doing math calculations in his head.

"*Big, big* flowers. Minimum a hundred dollars a pop. Last year I bet it was a two-hundred-dollar arrangement."

"Really!" he said, the energy rapidly draining from his voice and being replaced by nervous irritability. "Well, great. Great. That's just great. Hmm."

He paused again.

"So. Anything else new?"

He was totally distracted now. I could hear him composing an irate speech to deliver to his assistant. I wondered if she would get fired over this.

"Well, no. Not much else new going on," I told him. "Just thought I'd thank you in person for seven years of really amazing floral centerpieces. They were very impressive. I couldn't really get over how elaborate and expensive some of them were," I continued, deciding to rub it in.

"Hey, you're welcome. I'm so glad you enjoyed them," he said. Apparently the flowers had rendered him speechless.

We yammered pointlessly a little while longer and then we hung up. The rest of the day I teeter-tottered between feeling really melancholy and giggling uncontrollably.

What I Learned This Year:

1. No more trying to decipher the secret code of others. From now on, take everyone at face value, period. If it seems like there is something complex that I suspect may be in code, remember that the person who is making me feel that way is being an asshole. If I can't understand what they're saying, too bad for them. I can't do all the work. My brain pathways are in exile.

2. No more worrying about the Hole. To hell with the Hole. There *is* no Hole. I made it up. And I tiptoed around it long enough.

    If I want to worry about something all the time, try to remember there are bigger, more important things to worry about. For example, Y2K, which, experts say, is going to screw up civilization in a really big way starting in about a year. I've got to remember to buy a two-week supply of canned carrots, salt-free soup, SpaghettiOs, low-sodium chili . . . foods that I hate, so that I won't eat them when I wake up starving in the middle of the night.

3. See Dad as a yogic experiment in learning how to cope.

4. Don't be sorry that Mike is gone because clearly if we had continued on together, he would have started cheating. And if there is one thing I do not want to turn out to be, it is a delusional love chump who will put up with absolutely anything anyone forces on her, like Hillary Clinton.

5. If I am going to keep living in a fantasy world, work on developing a more impressive fantasy.

What I Hope to Learn in the Coming Year:

No more about quantum physics now that I read the quote by Nobel Prize–winning quantum physicist Richard Feynman, who said, "I think I can safely say that nobody understands quantum mechanics." If nobody gets it, what in the world do I think I am doing? No, it is time to pick a brand-new unfathomable area.

So . . . maybe something, anything, about French cooking or cars.